THE LONG WIRE

Barry Cord

CENTER POINT LARGE PRINT
THORNDIKE, MAINE

This Center Point Large Print edition
is published in the year 2019 by arrangement with
Golden West Literary Agency.

First US edition: Ace Books

The text of this Large Print edition is unabridged.
In other aspects, this book may vary
from the original edition.

Set in 16-point Times New Roman type.

ISBN: 978-1-64358-134-7 (hardcover)
ISBN: 978-1-64358-138-5 (paperback)

Library of Congress Cataloging-in-Publication Data

Names: Cord, Barry, 1913–1983, author.
Title: The long wire / Barry Cord.
Description: Center Point Large Print edition. | Thorndike, Maine :
    Center Point Large Print, 2019.
Identifiers: LCCN 2018059298| ISBN 9781643581347
    (hardcover : alk. paper) | ISBN 9781643581385
    (paperback : alk. paper)
Subjects: LCSH: Telegraph lines—Design and construction—
    Fiction. | Large type books.
Classification: LCC PS3505.O6646 L66 2019 | DDC 813/.54—dc23
LC record available at https://lccn.loc.gov/2018059298

Printed and bound in Great Britain
by TJ International Ltd, Padstow, Cornwall

MIX
Paper from
responsible sources
FSC
www.fsc.org   FSC® C013056

THE
LONG
WIRE

I

The fire-gutted ruins of the old ranch house showed like blackened bones through the thin grove of cottonwoods. Beyond the grown-over corn field behind the house the slope pitched steeply upward, breaking against the sheer face of Frenchman's Canyon.

"The bluff's our only obstacle," Davis said. "We lick that and we've got a fifty mile shortcut. That's a week off our completion schedule."

His companion, a thin man with an old face, shrugged. "The bluff isn't all we have to lick, Bill. There's old Frenchy's ghost—"

Davis interrupted with a snort. "Don't tell me the stories got to you, too, Steve?"

Steve Orville, timekeeper and assistant to Bill Davis, construction foreman for the Trans-Pecos Telegraph Company, smiled wryly. "Must be something to it," he insisted. "Take a real close look. Good spot for a ranch—natural grazing, good soil. But nobody's taken over since that Frenchman hung himself—"

Davis shook his head. He was a rough-hewn, blunt man in his late thirties, a good construction boss and a practical man. He did not believe in ghosts.

"Frenchy's ghost or not," he growled, "we're

stringing wire through this canyon. We'll lay twenty-five poles to the mile, and string it free up the bluff until we can work out better supports. We've got a time schedule to meet and by hell we'll meet it. I promised Mr. Simpson we could do it—"

He turned and glanced at Steve, who looked troubled. "Look, Steve," he said slowly, "it won't be Frenchy's ghost who'll give us trouble. I saw Mike Donovan in town. He wasn't exactly pleased when Trans-Pecos beat Overland out of the bid on this job. I know Mike, and if we run into trouble I know who'll be behind it!"

Steve shrugged. "It's still a long jump to Fort Cochise." He glanced up to the clouds edging the sky over the bluff. "We'll be running into rainy weather any day. We'll be lucky if we make it before the ground starts to freeze—"

Davis cut him off. "We'll make it!" he said grimly. "If I have to work the pole setters day and night. We'll string that wire to Cochise on time or Trans-Pecos folds. Reckon that ain't no secret," he added bitterly.

Steve shook his head. "Guess it isn't," he admitted. He glanced up at the threatening sky again. "Let's get back to camp, Bill."

They swung away. The afternoon sun was low over the eastern rim of the canyon, shooting its rays under the cloud mass. The road back brought them in close to the eastern rim where mesquite

8

and thorn shrubs clung to the friable slope. An old miner's cabin leaned on a shelf of stone, long deserted, its glassless window peering like a dark eye on the trail below.

They jogged on. The wind rose now and up among the jumbled rocks it was twisted and buffeted until it set up a high, tortured wailing, like some mortal in agony.

Steve licked his lips. "I'll be glad when we get through here, Bill. They say that Frenchy—"

He heard the foreman grunt and turned to see the construction boss slap at the side of his neck. "Damn gnats!" Bill said. He caught the look on Steve's white face and laughed. "Cripes!" he jeered. "You look like you spotted Frenchy's ghost—"

Steve took a deep breath. "You sure scared me," he admitted. "I thought—"

He felt the sting at the back of his neck and his motion was reflexive. He slapped at it and felt something small and hard roll against his fingers; he looked down on the ground below him, but didn't see anything.

But an unknown fear suddenly gripped at his bowels with icy fingers.

"Damn, let's get out of here," he muttered, and touched spurs to his cayuse.

Bill Davis laughed. "Hey, wait for me!" He rode quickly, catching up to Steve within a quarter of a mile. The mouth of the canyon was ahead of them, and the construction camp was less than five miles beyond this point, along the south bank of Cottonwood Creek.

"Steve, wait . . ." Bill felt suddenly tired, unable to breathe. He put his hands around the saddle horn to hold on. He saw Steve turn to face him. The timekeeper was swaying in his saddle. Suddenly he tilted sidewise, away from Bill, and fell. . . .

Davis kneed his horse up close. Steve was on his back, he seemed to be fighting for air. His mouth was open and his eyes were wide, distorted with agony.

Fear twisted its knife in Davis' gut. He turned his horse away and raked its flanks. He tried to cling to the saddle horn, but the horse's gallop jolted him loose. He fell less than four hundred yards from Steve Orville.

The two horses drifted slowly back toward the construction camp. By sundown Moss Sevart, night telegrapher, saw them grazing along the Cottonwood. He rounded up some men and rode back.

They found Bill Davis' body first, and later, Steve's. There wasn't a mark on either man they could see. But they were dead. As dead as any man could be.

One of the construction workers looked down the darkening canyon. The wind up along Organ

Rock made its deep-toned wail of despair. They shivered.

"Frenchy's ghost for sure. I ain't working through here—"

They brought the bodies back to camp. The night operator, his face white, tapped out a message to Paul Saint, Trans-Pecos Division Manager in Junction City, twenty-one miles away.

Then he came out of the tent and looked down at the bodies. "Can't understand it," he said. "Looks like they strangled to death. But there isn't a mark on them."

"Someone strangled them, all right!" Murdock, a wire stringer, said. "Frenchy's hands . . ." He stepped back from the bodies and looked into the darkness, toward Frenchy's Canyon. "I didn't want to work in that canyon in the first place. If Trans-Pecos is set on building through there, I'm quitting!" He looked around, his face flushing. "I'll string wire with any man here!" he snarled. "I've strung wire in a blizzard and in rainstorms! But I draw the line at stringing wire in a dead man's canyon!"

The muttering that rose from the other men leaned in his favor.

The night telegrapher shrugged. "Mr. Saint is sending a doctor out. We'll just sit right here, until we get further orders. . . ."

II

The thin rain came swirling down between the day coaches to spray the big man who lurched out to the small platform. He put his back to the wet door and took a deep breath; his eyes were small and bloodshot under knuckle-scarred brows.

"Gotta sober up quick," he thought dismally. "Can't walk into the Trans-Pecos office looking like this."

He wasn't drunk. But he knew he had been hired on as construction chief for Trans-Pecos with the condition that he leave the whiskey bottle alone.

"I can use a man like you," Warren Simpson had told him. Mr. Simpson was the big boss of Trans-Pecos. "I want that wire through to Fort Cochise on schedule. You can do it for me, Evans—if you'll lay off the bottle!"

Walter Evans put a calloused palm to his craggy features and scrubbed them. He was a burly, thick-shouldered man—a brawling, two-fisted individual who had started out as a pole-setter with Overland Telegraph and worked his way up to construction boss—and then drank his way out of the job.

The chill wind revived him somewhat after the stale tobacco fumes of the smoker. He studied the rugged terrain flanking the railbed with a wire-stringer's eye. The train was picking up speed on a downgrade, making a long curve between rock-studded hills. The smoke of the big Mallet engine up front whipped back over the coaches, thick with cinders.

Be in Junction City in fifteen minutes, he thought. This was his chance to get back on his feet. It wouldn't be like working for Overland or Western Pacific. Trans-Pecos was a small, independent outfit. Purely a Texas outfit. Sooner or later Western Union would swallow Trans-Pecos. The big man had seen it happen to Pacific Telegraph and Overland.

Trans-Pecos would break itself trying to fulfill its contract on time. A wire to Fort Myers and Cochise, up in wild rugged terrain. When it was strung Western Union would step in and buy Trans-Pecos out . . . or take over the line when Trans-Pecos went bankrupt.

Walt Evans shrugged. He had no real loyalty for Trans-Pecos. But Warren Simpson had hired him when no one else would even consider him for a pole-setter's job. Hired him on as construction chief for the company. Walt licked his lips. There was a catch in it somewhere. But he was thankful for the job.

He reached inside his back pocket for the flask he carried, shook it. Not more than one good swallow left. No sense wasting it. He hesitated only briefly, then uncapped it and brought it to his lips.

He saw the rider then as the railbed curved in close to a road snaking through the hills. A young man on a big black horse with four white stockings—an easy-riding man covered by a poncho. They topped the trail some fifty feet above the railbed. The man waved in friendly gesture, then the curving train pulled Evans away from the road and the rider.

Evans finished his drink and tossed the flask away. He wiped his lips, feeling the dampness soak through his new suit coat. The door to his coach opened and two men came out to the jolting platform. Walt had seen them before. They had gotten aboard at Verne's Pass, the last stop.

One was tall and somewhat cadaverous-looking. A man with long arms, hairy hands and a dull, horsey face. The other was shorter, wiry, with a small round face on which nose, mouth and eyes were bunched together. Both men were dressed in ill-fitting store clothes.

They seemed about to pass through to the next car. The taller man suddenly eased his back against the door and the wiry man turned and tapped Evans on the arm.

"Got a match, Mr. Evans?"

Walt nodded. "Sure have." He reached into his pocket and the muzzle that prodded his side stiffened him. He didn't have time to think. The gun blast twisted him around, his face shocked into a mask of pain. The taller man jammed his palm into Evans' face and the construction boss fell backward. Blind instinct made him reach for the handbar.

He clung there, vaguely conscious of the clicking, deadly wheels below him. The smaller man's gun blasted again. Evans' grip loosened and he fell backward. A tiny warning flickering in his head made him jump at the last moment.

He landed heavily on loose earth and gravel and slid down the rail embankment into thick bushes which halted his descent. He lay for a few moments in a gray world of pain. The rain fell softly on his upturned face.

He knew he was dying. He rolled over and started to crawl. Dimly he remembered the trail flanking the roadbed, remembered the rider who had waved. He kept crawling, blindly, until his strength gave out.

The train swept past, going into an S-bend down the desolate slope. The tall man gripped the handbar and leaned way out, trying to spot Evans. But the curve of the train hid the spot where the Trans-Pecos construction boss had fallen.

"Better make sure of him, Pete," he said harshly. "We don't want anyone finding him still alive."

Pete shrugged. He eyed the weather and there

was distaste in his regard. But he knew better than to argue with the taller man.

He stepped down the iron ladder and waited, judging the speed of the train and picking out a soft spot. Then he jumped. He landed and rolled, skinning his knees and the palms of his hands. He cursed grimly.

The tall man waved to him. Pete flattened down behind the wet bushes as the rear of the train swung past; he didn't want anyone to see him. The windows were rain-streaked and blurred— the coaches swept by and then the train was gone. The flat, lonely sound of its whistle, announcing its arrival to Junction City only minutes away, came back to him.

Pete drew his gun and headed back up the tracks, looking for Evans. . . .

Jim Davis heard the shots whip on the wind: faint pops that drifted up to him through the rain.

He reined his black stud in to the side of the road, the rain sifting against his poncho. There was an autumn chill in the rain and the slope was gray and dismal under the lowering sky.

He leaned forward over the horn, peering between two huge boulders and he could see the train moving like some dull black sidewinder over the curving steel rails below. Smoke lay thick and black over the coaches.

Davis ran his gaze to the platform of the third

car where he had seen the big man and surprise etched a small furrow above his cold gray eyes. The big man was gone. But there were two other men there now, a tall man and a short one. And even as he looked the smaller man jumped.

Then the train curved away, around a rock outcrop, and the flat mournful whistle lay heavy on the air.

Davis studied the scene for a long moment, a hardness in his eyes. He was twenty-five, but he looked older, harder. He had knocked around a good deal since he and his brother had split up five years before, and the interval had put a cynical glint behind the coldness in his eyes.

His brother had been working for Western Pacific then. "You know this business as well as I do," he had told Jim. "But you're old enough to find out what you really want to do with your life. Go ahead—get it out of your system. When you're ready, come back. I'll have a job for you."

He had seen his brother once in those five years, a brief meeting at Promontory Point during a celebration of Union Pacific. His brother Bill was the same, but Jim had changed . . . he knew it and Bill knew it and Bill had said goodbye when Jim left.

"You won't be coming back," he had told Jim. "In a way, I'm sorry. I hope you find out what you really want to do some day." They had shaken hands. "Keep in touch, kid," Bill had said.

But the next time Jim heard from his brother he was dead.

He swung the big restless black horse away from the edge of the road and rode slowly until he found an opening off trail. He rode the black down here, heading for the railbed.

Part way down the slope the horse shied away from something ahead. Jim came out of the saddle and walked to the man who lay face down in a small clearing between the rocks.

Walt Evans had crawled almost a hundred feet upslope from the rails. He had clawed the earth in a blind effort to live, an organism that moved only because movement was a part of life. He was still breathing when Jim crouched over him.

But Davis saw immediately there was nothing he could do for this man. He listened to Evans' agonized breathing for a moment, then the slide of a man's boot on rain-slickened rock jerked his head around.

His hand reached under his poncho for his holstered Colt; he was remembering the wiry man who had jumped from the train a few minutes before. . . .

Pete came into view a few moments later. He was following Evans' trail up the slope, a shallow groove in the wet earth seemingly made by some giant slug. Pete's gun was held ready in his hand. He came around the wet rocks and froze, eyeing Jim crouched beside Evans' now still body.

Jim Davis said grimly, "You should have remained on the train, Mac. He's dead!"

Pete's gun muzzle came up and he thumbed a quick shot at Jim. But Jim's fire spun him around. He stumbled and slipped, plunging headfirst against a nearby boulder.

Jim flinched at the gory splat. Rising, he walked slowly over to Pete and turned the limp figure over. Pete's bloody head rolled loosely.

Davis had shot only to wound the man, but it was Pete's bad luck that he had fallen and smashed his head against the rock. Jim squatted by the small man and went through his pockets, looking for identification.

He found the usual personal items the man carried, but nothing to indicate who he was. Yet there was two hundred dollars in the man's wallet in crisp new twenty dollar bills. This was something a man did not usually carry.

Davis walked back to Evans. The construction boss had little on him. A few dollars, a watch with a heavy gold chain. Inside the back watch cover was an engraved message: *To Walter Evans, in grateful appreciation, from Overland Telegraph.*

Jim pocketed the watch. His face held a small frown as he searched the dead man's coat pockets.

He found a letter in an inside pocket and read it with interest.

It was addressed to Paul Saint, Division Head, Trans-Pecos Telegraph Company, Junction City, Texas. It read:

Dear Paul: This will introduce Walter Evans, your new construction boss. He's worked for Overland and for Western Pacific for years. He's rough and bull-headed, but he knows wire. If you can keep him off the bottle he'll get our line through on schedule. I don't have to remind you how important it is that we hook up with Fort Myers before October first. I'm negotiating for more time on the loan and will have supplies you requested shipped to you by weekend. Will see you personally before the end of October.

It was signed by Warren Simpson, head of Trans-Pecos and there was a P.S. "No time to survey new route. Keep to original plan. I'm sending a troubleshooter to look into Ghost Canyon."

Jim Davis folded the letter and returned it to the envelope. He stood in the lee of the boulder, his face hard, a plan taking shape in him.

Trans-Pecos and his brother's death were the

reasons he was here now, on his way to Junction City.

He had come back from Mexico too late to attend Bill's funeral. But he had gone into see Mr. Simpson; he wanted to know how Bill had died.

"You'll have to ask Paul Saint," Simpson had told him. "All I know is that your brother was surveying a route through Ghost Canyon—they call it Frenchman's Canyon, too. It would have cut more than thirty-five miles from the original plan." Simpson made a weary gesture. "He was found dead at the mouth of the canyon."

Jim said grimly, "Bill have enemies?"

Simpson shrugged. "None that I knew of." He smiled wryly. "But I have. Business enemies." He studied the hard man standing before him. "You want a job with Trans-Pecos?"

"I want to know how my brother died," Jim said thinly.

Warren Simpson came to his feet. "Maybe you can find that out, and do me a favor besides." He walked up to a wall map showing Trans-Pecos lines. "All I've gotten from my division manager is a lot of gibberish about a ghost killer in Frenchy's Canyon. My construction crews are at a standstill. Paul Saint wants permission to string wire along another route. This one." His finger traced a route on the map. "It'll add at least a week to my completion time." He turned to Jim. "I can't afford the delay. Your brother Bill knew it. That's why he planned to go through that canyon . . ."

He paused, waiting for Jim to say something. Jim nodded slowly. "What do you want me to do, Mr. Simpson?"

"Find out what's going on down there. I've already hired a new construction chief, a man named Walter Evans." Simpson walked back to his desk, turned. "Shall I wire Paul Saint you're coming?"

Jim shook his head. "I'll go in on my own. Later, I'll check in with your new construction boss." He shrugged. "All I want is to find out how my brother died."

"Suit yourself," Simpson said. He had sounded disappointed.

Jim remembered this now as he looked down at Evans' body. He hated to leave the dead man here. But if he brought Evans in to Junction City he'd be tying himself to a lot of explanations he didn't want to get into.

And it was apparent someone was out to break Trans-Pecos. They had killed Evans, and it was more than likely now they had killed his brother Bill.

Jim walked back to his horse and mounted. He stared off through the rain-misted hills. The wail of the locomotive pulling into Junction City drifted back to him, faint on the chill wind.

"I'll give Trans-Pecos a hand, Bill," he said softly. "I guess I owe you this much."

The big black snorted and moved out at the touch of his heels.

III

Junction City was not at its best when Jim Davis saw it. He rode into town along a wet trail that flanked the rails most of the way. Rain swept in squalls across the dingy wooden depot and over the ugly frame buildings clustered beyond the freight yards.

A switcher was jogging boxcars in the yards, working like some panting, tired animal. But the passenger train Jim had seen earlier had already left Junction City. A man in shirt-sleeves was on the awning-protected platform, checking over baggage piled on a hand truck.

Jim swung his attention to the buggy heading for him. The man hunched over the reins was tall and cadaverous. He shot Jim a quick look as the younger man reined aside to let him roll past.

Jim's gaze narrowed and he turned to look after the buggy disappearing in the rain. This man was one of the two he had seen on the train platform, after Evans had disappeared.

Probably heading back to pick up his friend, Jim thought coldly and the reflection relieved him of responsibility for the two dead men.

He turned his horse down Center Street, seeking out a stable and a hotel. He found the hotel first—a square, three-decker frame structure with

24

a huge board sign nailed above the wide porch: TEXAS HOTEL.

He passed it by, riding until another board sign with a painted hand signal indicated the Ace Stables down a narrow alleyway. Jim left the black stud and instructions with a hostler and came back through the mud of the alley carrying his warbag.

He walked through the slackening rain to the hotel, protected on this side of the street by a board awning. There was a considerable amount of foot traffic on the walks but no one paid much attention to the poncho-clad man among them. Jim turned in at the hotel, a sooty structure close to the freight yard, its curlicued facade making a pretense at grandeur it did not possess.

He walked inside, signed at the desk and went upstairs with the habitual softness of a big, wary cat. He rounded the landing and was several steps down the dimly lighted hallway when he saw the two figures in close embrace in a doorway.

"I'll do it, Ellen. Anything you say. Just don't—"

They pushed apart as Jim Davis came up. The girl looked at him, a cool arrogance in her gaze. Instinctively she put a hand to her hair to pat it in place.

Jim put a casual glance on the flush-faced man, noting that he was young, hardly more than a boy. He was wearing town clothes, a blue-striped shirt with a celluloid collar, and there was enough red in his hair to explain the sudden belligerence with which he eyed Jim.

The woman was at least five years older. Jim caught a whiff of heliotrope as he walked by. A mature woman, not too ruffled by being caught in a somewhat compromising situation.

Jim dropped his warbag in front of his door and unlocked it. He glanced back and noticed that the girl was gone. The youngster was still in his doorway, eyeing him with tight-mouthed anger.

Hell, Jim thought sourly, *it isn't any of my business. Wonder what's got you so riled?*

The youngster slammed the door and Jim grinned and went inside his room. The shade was pulled down the length of the lone window and the bleakness of the day made it even more gloomy inside. He raised the shade and stared around the room, noting the last occupant must have been politically minded. Several posters were tacked to the walls, all requesting that the voter of Cochise County vote for the "Honorable, upright and capable Vic Collins" for sheriff.

Jim wondered idly if Collins had been elected.

He shucked his wet clothes, washed, and got into dry trousers and shirt. He eyed the cartridge belt he had tossed onto the bed. The plain leather holster showed some wear and the walnut butt of the Colt .45 had the patina of use. It was just as well, he thought, that Bill didn't know what he had done in those five years.

He picked up the cartridge belt, but then decided against wearing it. It did not fit in with the character of Walt Evans, a capable construction boss, but no gunman. So he stowed the belt away, thrust the gun in his waistband, and buttoned his coat over it.

He cocked his hat back on his head and glanced into the mirror. The face that looked back at him had been shaped by the sun and weather of a thousand lonely trails. It was a face honed lean by trouble, yet saved from grimness by the touch of wry humor at the corners of his mouth.

It was not a drinker's face. He remembered Walt's face, craggy, dotted around the nose and high cheeks with the tiny hemorrhaged capillaries. *Might pass,* he thought bleakly, *if no one here knows Walt.*

The men who had killed Evans must have known he was coming to Junction City, but it did not necessarily mean they knew Evans personally. They may have been tipped off that the new Trans-Pecos construction boss was on his way and struck up an acquaintance with him on the train. Or asked the conductor. If so, Jim had a chance of making the deception stick—at least long enough to get a good look at what was going on here.

He turned to the rain-smeared window and

looked out over the roofs. From Junction City the mountains loomed sharp on clear days—they were hidden in the storm clouds now.

He turned and left the room, locking it behind him. The youngster's door was closed as he went past it.

He paused in the lobby to ask the desk clerk directions to the Trans-Pecos division office. The youngster he had seen upstairs with the woman was now in a chair in the lobby, behind a newspaper. He glanced at Jim with quick interest as the clerk gave directions, and buried his face in the newspaper again when Jim turned to look at him.

Davis went outside and paused for a moment under the hotel awning. The rain was slackening to a drizzle. But the afternoon was wearing away and the puddles in the street glittered in the light of the fading day. Wagons roiled the puddles and churned up the mud.

He headed for the depot. There were fewer people on the walks now, and when he crossed the street and took Railroad Avenue he became aware that he was being followed.

The late afternoon had turned just dark enough to blur things. He moved more quickly, cutting down along the rail yards. A switcher puffed past, steam billowing up and momentarily hiding Jim.

He took this opportunity to duck into a doorway. The switcher moved away and above

28

the hissing boiler he heard the thud of running feet. He waited until the pursuer was close, then Jim stepped out, caught the running man by the arm, and jerked him around.

Close up he saw that it was the redheaded youngster!

The kid gave a short yelp of surprise and swung a haymaker for Jim's face. Jim caught his arm, spun him around, and curled his right forearm under the boy's chin. His arm tightened and he lifted the youngster from the ground. He held him writhing, struggling, until he felt the boy weaken. Then he eased him down, jerked him around and pinned him against the closed door.

"What are you after?" Jim demanded coldly.

The youngster massaged his throat, his eyes sullen. "I wasn't following you—"

Jim's fingers tightened and he lifted the boy up on his toes, his eyes narrowing. "You run in the rain for fun?"

The other gulped. "I heard you ask for Trans-Pecos at the desk. I thought you might be hired by Paul Saint to spy on his sister." He was faintly defiant. "I don't want to cause her any trouble. She's not—she's not what Paul would think—"

"You thought I was on my way to report what I had seen in the hallway?" Jim released his hold on the boy. "How old are you?"

"Twenty," the boy said. "I'm Dick Rainer,

timekeeper for the Trans-Pecos construction crew at Cottonwood Creek camp."

Jim frowned. "What are you doing in town?"

"No reason why I shouldn't be here," Rainer replied angrily. "Crew's just laying around, waiting for orders." He was regaining his confidence. "I got sick of camp and came here." He leered at Jim. "Who in the devil are you, anyway?"

"Walt Evans," Jim answered bluntly. "Trans-Pecos' new construction boss."

"Oh!" Confusion flickered across the youngster's face. "I—I heard we were getting a new man—"

"Get back to the hotel!" Jim ordered. "I'll pick you up in the morning."

"Yes . . . yes, sir!" Dick nodded. He picked up his hat. "Sorry about this, Mr. Evans. I thought—"

"See you in the morning," Jim cut him off.

The youngster ducked into the rain and disappeared around the corner.

Jim stared after him. At least this boy didn't know Evans. It was a start. . . .

IV

Trans-Pecos' division office was on Second Street. It was a long, narrow one-story building with a warehouse in back and a wagon yard. Although it was not yet five o'clock, there were lights burning in the office.

Jim pushed open the door and found himself in a waiting room fenced off from several desks by a low walnut stained railing. A sallow-faced man was hunched over a telegraph key, listening intently to rapid clicks from a receiving instrument.

At the desk across from this man Paul Saint was frowning. Paul was a handsome, well built man, about thirty, with a pencil-line moustache and cool gray eyes. He glanced once at Jim and dismissed him as of lesser importance. He leaned forward as the operator turned and said nervously, "That was Casey, Mr. Saint. He says that last wagonload of poles never got to camp. They found Morgan and the poles at the bottom of Shawlee's Slide."

"I read him!" Paul Saint interrupted coldly. He turned and looked up at Jim now, a cold antagonism in his regard.

"What can I do for you, sir?" he asked curtly.

Jim glanced at the girl standing by the file cabinet. She was cleaning her nails. Her hair was brown, with bronze highlights. She returned his look with a provocative smile, as though she were daring him to say something concerning the incident he had witnessed in the hotel.

Jim said, "I'm Walt Evans. Your new construction boss."

Paul started. He came to the railing, his eyes searching Jim's face. "Evans?" His voice held a sharp distrust. "Mr. Simpson wired me you were coming. But—"

Jim handed him the letter he had taken from Evans.

Paul Saint read it slowly, then handed it back. "I thought you'd be in on the late train today," he said. "I was at the depot when it pulled in—"

"I rode in," Jim said. "My horse is at the stable."

"Oh!" Paul Saint shrugged. He turned to the girl by the cabinet. "My sister, Ellen Saint," he introduced. "She helps me out with the book work, Mr. Evans."

Ellen Saint smiled. "We've met, Paul. Not formally, however." She came up and offered Jim her hand. It was soft, but firm in Jim's grasp; there was certainty in her handshake. "So you're the man Simpson expects to do the impossible,

32

Mr. Evans? You have our support, of course—and my condolences."

"Condolences?"

Paul flushed. "Don't mind my sister, Walt. She has a cynical outlook about everything in Texas. Coming from the East, she doesn't like this part of the country, nor the people."

"How wrong you are, Paul," Ellen cut in tartly. "The country has its points of interest, and some of the men I've met are gallant. But I'm speaking as an employee of Trans-Pecos. I think we're licked on this one, Paul—and if you were honest with me, you'd admit it, too."

Paul shrugged and turned away from her. His lips held a slight pouting. "My job is cost sheets and supply, Walt. Not construction. And I can't make men work when they're afraid."

"Afraid of what?"

Paul cast a quick glance at the operator. He opened the gate in the railing, said, "Come in, Walt. Sit down. I thought Mr. Simpson told you what to expect."

Jim found a chair and sat down. Paul remained on his feet; his face was troubled. "I'll give it to you straight, then. I don't think you can get that line up to Cochise in time. Not with that fifty mile detour staring us in the face."

"We're going through Ghost Canyon," Jim said. "Those were Mr. Simpson's orders."

Paul stiffened. "Simpson's a fool!" he snapped.

33

"The men won't work through that canyon. Not after what happened to Bill Davis and Orville."

"What happened to them?"

Paul made an unhappy gesture with his hands. "Nobody knows, really. Except that Davis and Orville are dead. And Kemp Overton. Bill Davis was the construction boss before you. I'm sure Simpson told you?" Jim nodded. "Davis and Orville were making a survey through the canyon," Paul went on, "marking sites for the pole setters. They didn't come back. But their horses did. Some of the men at camp went into the canyon and found Davis and Orville. Looked like they had fallen off their horses. No sign of anything wrong. No marks, no bullet wounds. But they were dead. The town doctor is still confused. Strangled, he says. They just stopped breathing—like someone took them by the neck and choked them. Only he left no marks."

Paul looked steadily at Jim. "Kemp Overton was the next man to die. He rode into the canyon out of curiosity, I imagine. He was found like Davis and Orville—he had died the same way. The sheriff took a posse out and scoured the canyon. They didn't find a thing"—Paul smiled—"a living thing, that is."

"There's a quaint legend about that canyon," Ellen Saint put in. "Back about twelve years ago it was a ranch called the *Bon Ami*. A Frenchman from New Orleans who some say was the black sheep son of a French count had settled there with a pretty young wife. One day he surprised his wife with the hired hand. He killed them both and then hung himself from the barn rafters. The legend claims it's his ghost that haunts the canyon."

Jim shrugged. "Have you been in the canyon?"

"Several times." Ellen's smile was roguish. "I am not afraid of ghosts, Mr. Evans, and I sometimes find myself in sympathy with Madame Le Garant—"

"My sister is a bit too trusting," Paul Saint bit out coldly. There was a heavy layer of resentment in his voice.

Jim came to his feet. "Perhaps some day you'll ride with me to Ghost Canyon, Miss Saint?"

"If you wish." Interest danced in her eyes. "I see that you, too, are not afraid of ghosts."

"I've found them to be harmless," Jim smiled. "Some time tomorrow, if the weather lets up, I want to take a look in that canyon."

Paul's eyes held a stony cast. "I'll drive you out first thing in the morning. Work camp's over by Cottonwood Creek, about twenty miles from town. Jack Sanders is in charge. He was Bill Davis' assistant. Jack's a good man, but not tough enough for the job. It takes a strong

35

hand to push that crew, and Jack's not that kind."

Jim pushed the railing gate open. "Thanks, Mr. Saint. But I promised to ride out to camp with Dick Rainer."

He saw the quick look the girl put on him. Paul's face held a sharp surprise. "You've met Rainer?"

"In the hotel," Jim answered. "We found we had things in common."

"How nice!" Ellen Saint exclaimed. There was a teasing defiance in her eyes. "That you and young Rainer should like the same things, I mean."

There was an indirect invitation in her voice and in her eyes and Jim put a long look on her. Paul Saint came between them, his face dark and unfriendly.

"I'll ride out with you anyway, Walt," he said flatly. "I want to hear what happened at Shawlee's Slide from Jack Sanders."

Ellen Saint laughed. "Men always talk of work. It's the women who have to think of the social graces." She walked up to Jim and tucked her arm under his.

"Tomorrow you start work for Trans-Pecos, Walt. But tonight—will you take me out to dinner?"

"I should like that very much," Jim said. There was in him a bleak amusement at Paul Saint's hardlipped silence. And a sharpened interest in the telegraph line's division manager.

For Paul Saint was a jealous man—more jealous than a man had a right to be over a sister. . . .

V

The Eldorado was Junction City's most posh eating place, where the better-heeled and more refined of taste sought a leisurely, well-cooked meal accompanied by vintage wine. It had pretensions and an atmosphere over-stressed by the huge wall mural on the north side of the dining room depicting *Conquistador* Cortez at the head of a mounted column, marching across a sunlit plain to the walled city of the mythical Cibola.

Jim led Ellen to a corner table where a candle flickered in a green glass holder. It had been a long time since he had taken a beautiful woman to dinner, and Ellen Saint was a strikingly beautiful woman.

He wondered what had brought her to this western railroad town. She had the gloss of the East on her; she did not appear to be the kind of woman who would stay on here.

He helped her with her chair and sat down opposite her. The candle glow touched his face and she leaned forward, slipping her gloves from her hands. "You surprise me, Mr. Evans. From what I heard of you I expected a"—she smiled to soften her statement—"more uncouth man."

Jim shrugged. "Gossip tends to exaggeration." He did not wish to talk of Walter Evans, but she pressed the conversation.

"Paul heard of you," she said. "When we got word you were coming we expected—well, we expected trouble. Even Mr. Simpson mentioned that you were a—a hard drinker, to put it mildly."

"I've reformed," Jim said dryly.

"So it seems." She settled back, smiling. "I hope what you saw in the hallway today doesn't bother you, Mr. Evans?"

"Should it?"

She shrugged. "I'm thinking of Paul. He's . . . well, you know how protective some men are toward their sisters?"

Jim's smile had a touch of cynicism. "If you're asking me to keep my mouth shut, you don't have to. My concern is with Trans-Pecos."

He turned as the waiter came up and took their order. "Mr. Simpson gave me a job when no one else in the business would," he continued after the waiter left. "I'd like to get that wire strung through to Cochise on time for him."

She shook her head. "Impossible. Even going through Ghost Canyon it would have been cutting it close." She eyed him speculatively. "I can appreciate your reasons for wanting to help Trans-Pecos. But after what's happened, none of the Trans-Pecos crew is willing to work in that canyon."

"I think they'll work," Jim said evenly. "I happen to be a very stubborn man."

They ate in a cool silence after that and he escorted her back to the house where the Saints lived and left her at the gate.

"I'll see you and your brother in the morning," he said.

He walked back to the hotel and went up to his room. Light seeping under his closed door alerted him. He paused, eyes narrowing. He had turned down the light and locked the door before going out.

He hesitated, his hand on the knob, remembering that he had left his gun in the room, not wanting to take it with him to dinner.

From inside a heavy voice said, "Come in . . . come in."

Jim opened the door and stepped inside.

The man standing by the bed was big, burly; he seemed too big for his town clothes. He was about forty, graying a little, like a weathered oak stump, and seemingly as solid.

"Heard you outside," he said. He did not seem in the least concerned that Jim's warbag was open on the bed. He was holding Evans' gold watch by the chain, twirling it slowly. He made a motion toward a chair.

"Sit down," he said.

Jim shook his head. "You seem to be in the wrong room, mister—"

"Donovan—Mike Donovan." The big man smiled. "You're Walter Evans?"

"The name's in the register," Jim said coldly.

"I know what you wrote in the register," the big man said. "But you're not Evans." He tossed the watch down on the bed. "I fired Walt two years ago," he said casually. "A good man, but he drank too much."

There was no use pretending with this man, Jim saw. He said coldly, "What do you want?"

"I happen to be with Overland Telegraph," Mike said softly. "And we want this contract. Trans-Pecos took the bid from us." He shrugged. "We don't mind. Simpson'll break himself trying to string his wire to Cochise on schedule. We expect to take it over when he does."

"What if Trans-Pecos builds through on schedule?"

"You won't!" Donovan's eyes took on a frosty glint. "That's why I'm here. I don't know who you are or what your game is, and I don't care. Long as you see that Trans-Pecos doesn't get through on time."

He took an expensive cigar from his coat pocket, extended one to Jim.

"You're the new construction boss," he said, smiling. "You can make sure Trans-Pecos folds. And when that happens there'll be five thousand dollars waiting for you."

Jim grinned coldly. "You willing to put that in writing, Mr. Donovan?"

The big man's eyes glittered. "You have my word, no more."

Jim shook his head. "I think you've got me figured wrong. I'm not Walt Evans. But I'm going to see that Trans-Pecos gets through to Cochise. On time!"

Donovan moved his heavy shoulders. He looked more like a man used to roughhouse slugging than soft talk. "I don't know what happened to Walt. But—"

"Evans is dead," Jim cut in grimly.

Donovan eyed him for a beat. "Well, that makes it more interesting. Walt's dead, and you're in town passing yourself off in his place. Maybe the sheriff would like to know why!"

He walked to the door and looked back at Jim. "Think it over, fella. I'll give you until tomorrow night to make up your mind!"

VI

Lee Watson drove through the wet night, his thoughts angry and confused. In back of the buggy seat were the bodies of Pete and the man he thought was Walt Evans.

He had hired the buggy to pick up Pete, expecting to find the wiry man waiting for him along the trail. He had reached the spot where the Trans-Pecos construction boss had been hurled from the train, and only after half an hour of swearing and searching had he come upon the bodies.

It didn't make sense to him. The rain had washed out all tracks so that even a better man than Lee at reading sign would have had trouble making out what had happened.

He had found Pete dead. The wiry man had a bullet-gashed arm and his head was bashed in. Lee guessed that Pete had fallen against the boulder under which he lay.

Evans' body was further on, in the clearing. He was soaked. Lee had searched his pockets and found nothing on the big man to identify him. Standing, he had felt a chill run down his spine.

He remembered the poncho-clad man who had come riding into town just as he was leaving. Had this stranger something to do with the killing of Pete? If so, who was he?

The rain was soaking down around the collar of his slicker and it was getting too dark to see the trail. Cursing, he had hauled the bodies up to the road and managed to get them into the cramped space behind the seat. Something had gone wrong and he knew that the boss would not take this easy.

The rain slacked off as he neared town. He drove in past the depot and swung into the alley leading to the Trans-Pecos wagon yard. There was a light in the office and he turned in at the side door.

The night operator was sitting back in his chair, reading a paper. He looked up as Lee walked inside, nodded.

"Where's Mr. Saint?"

"Gone home."

Lee took a deep breath. He turned and went out again and wheeled the buggy out of the yard. He drove around to the small cottage where Paul Saint lived and tied up at the hitching post in front of the gate.

Paul Saint opened the door. He frowned as he recognized Lee Watson, shot a quick look past him to the dark, muddy road, said sharply, "Come in, damn it. Don't stand out there."

He whirled on the man as they stepped into the kitchen. "Where's Pete? I've got questions to ask both of you."

"Pete's dead!" Lee growled. "That's why I'm

here." He jerked a thumb over his shoulder. "He's in the buggy with a busted head."

Paul stiffened. "Dead? I thought you and Pete had an easy job. Kill Walt Evans!"

"We did!" Lee snarled. "Walter Evans is in that buggy out there, with Pete. He's deader 'n last year's blowflies!"

Paul's eyes glittered. "What are you trying to pull on me, Lee? Walter Evans walked into my office an hour ago. He's out having dinner with—with Ellen right now."

Lee made an impatient gesture with his hands. "Hell, I tell you we killed Evans. I heard the conductor call his name; he even answered to that name when we called him. He's dead. But so's Pete. That's what I can't figure out, Paul."

He recited grimly what had happened. "I went back to pick up Pete and found him dead."

Paul Saint's face took on a stony cast. "A man who called himself Evans came into my office a couple of hours ago. He handed me a letter of introduction from the big boss, Warren Simpson."

"Young feller, riding a black horse, four white stockings?"

Paul shrugged. "He didn't resemble the description I had heard of Evans," he admitted. "Quiet, but a hard man, able to take care of himself." Paul paced the room, his face angry. "If he isn't Evans, then who is he?"

45

"Some spy sent out by Mr. Simpson?" Lee volunteered.

The Trans-Pecos division manager sneered. "Could be. I don't think Simpson trusts me as well as he should." He laughed thinly. "It doesn't matter. A delay of another week or so and Trans-Pecos is bankrupt. There won't be a chance in hell of making Fort Cochise on time."

"What about this man? Want me to take care of him?"

Paul Saint considered. He said, "No. Not now."

"What about the bodies I got in the buggy?"

"Take them over to the sheriff's office," Paul advised. "Tell Collins you found Pete and the dead man on the trail. Make up any story you like. The rain will wash out any evidence. And I'll see to it that it sticks."

Lee shrugged.

"And keep out of sight for a few days," Paul warned, "in case he connects you with Pete. Ride up to Superstition Point and wait. I'll get in touch with you there."

Lee nodded. "Just don't wait too long," he said. He walked to the door, looked back. There was no hint of disrespect in his voice or in his face as he added, "Me and Pete rode a lot of trails together, Mr. Saint. I'd like to see that he gets a decent burial."

"I'll see to it," Paul promised.

Saint walked to the rain-streaked window and waited there after Lee Watson left. The night was dark and he could see nothing beyond the window, but he heard Watson ride off, the sound of his passage fading quickly.

The night was raw with the first chill riding in from the high peaks northward. But inside the small room it was warm, heated by the big oak log burning in the fireplace. It was a pleasant room with a floor to ceiling bookcase flanking the fireplace. The books were old friends to Paul Saint; he had read them all.

A vase from Japan, a stone axe from Java, some wild animal skins from Africa, added their exotic touches to this room made pleasant this night by the fragrance of wood smoke.

But Paul was troubled. He stood by the window, his thoughts turned inward, a cold anger in his eyes. He was a slender man, deceptive in appearance. Few men guessed that behind the soft, cultured exterior was a hard man, toughened physically and emotionally, and held in control by an iron will. He looked like a man who had led a sheltered life, but Paul Saint had wandered in many of the outlandish places of earth before coming here and he could take care of himself in times of trouble with a variety of weapons.

But his greatest asset was his patience. He had learned to wait when there was nothing else he could do but wait—and he had learned it well.

Outside, the rain had all but stopped. He could hear water dripping from the eaves and from the north a wind rose, hurrying the clouds southward.

He turned to glance at the clock on the mantelpiece. It was still too early for Ellen, but he could not discard his annoyance at her for inviting herself to dinner with the man who called himself Walt Evans.

He walked to the fireplace and reached for his pipe and tobacco on the mantelpiece. The briar bowl was from Ireland, but the stem was East African ivory, and he had bought the pipe in a small London shop, off Cobberly.

He started to walk back to the window, but he caught himself and turned away, not wanting Ellen to see him waiting for her. He crossed to the big chair by the fire and took down a book from the shelves flanking the fireplace and settled down to read.

He was surprised when, less than twenty minutes later, he heard Ellen's voice outside, at the gate. She sounded a bit cold saying good night to the new construction foreman and he guessed the evening had not gone the way she had expected.

After a long moment the door opened and Ellen entered. She headed directly for the stairs leading to her bedroom, but she paused as she saw Paul in the chair by the fire.

He looked at ease and untroubled, but Ellen knew him better than that.

"Oh!" she said. "I thought you might still be at the office."

Paul just looked at her. He took the pipe from his mouth. "You're home early," he said. There was a malicious edge to his tone. "What happened? Lose your charm, Ellen?"

She shrugged, not wanting to get into a game of words with him. She started for her room, but his voice stopped her.

"Wait!" He had not raised his voice, but it was an order and she knew it. She turned slowly.

He came up from his chair and crossed slowly to her; the fireplace was at his back now and the flickering flames only emphasized the shadows in his thin face.

He said, "Some day you'll make me kill you." He said it dispassionately, but Ellen knew he meant it and she shivered slightly.

She said, "Paul, I only wanted to—"

He took her arms and pulled her to him and kissed her. It was a hard, brutal kiss with no tenderness in it. It was a kiss substituting for a slap in the face: it was meant as a punishment.

She pulled away from him finally and slowly ran the back of her hand across her bruised lips.

He eyed her coldly. "Stay away from him," he ordered. "He isn't a boy like Dick Rainer."

Anger flared in Ellen's eyes. "I did it for you," she said bitterly. "After all, isn't that why I'm here—as your sister?"

"Yes," he admitted. "But there are limits—"

She interrupted him. "Limits? Where do you want me to stop, Paul? A goodnight kiss?" Her lips twisted bitterly. "I made a bargain with you. I intend to stick by it."

A flicker of contempt showed in his eyes. "You don't have to go into the gutter to keep it."

She studied him for a long moment. Then: "Thank you. You're always the gentleman, aren't you, Paul? Except with me."

She started to turn away. He grabbed her wrist. "What did you find out?"

She looked back into his face. "Not much, directly. But if you'll accept a woman's intuition—be careful. He's been around; he's no dumb construction worker you can easily fool—"

"Who is he?"

"I didn't find out." She took a breath. "But he isn't Walter Evans. I'm sure of that."

He let go of her wrist.

"I'll ride out to Cottonwood camp with him tomorrow. You stay here. I'll make your excuses."

It was an order. She nodded.

He called after her as she started up the stairs. "I'll be up later."

She turned. "Don't bother." Her voice was thin.

He watched her go out of sight on the landing, then turned and walked back to his chair.

He stared into the flickering flames. It didn't really matter who the new man was . . . it was too late to save Trans-Pecos.

VII

Morning had a gray, depressive cast to it. It had stopped raining but the wind had veered and now came slanting in from the west, bringing the cold from snow-capped peaks with it.

Jim Davis came down into the hotel dining room and found Dick Rainer waiting for him at a table. The boy looked subdued. He had a cup of coffee in front of him and nothing else.

As Jim sat down he said apologetically, "About last night, Mr. Evans—"

Jim cut him off. "We'll forget last night." He motioned to a waiter, then asked Dick, "Is that all you're having—coffee?"

Dick shrugged. "I'm not very hungry."

The waiter came over and Jim said, "Ham and eggs for two. And bring us a pot of coffee as soon as you can." The waiter went away and Jim looked at Dick. "It's a long ride to camp. You'll need something to warm you."

Dick's smile was uncertain. "Thanks, Mr. Evans."

Jim said, "What for?"

"For not firing me," Dick answered. And added hesitantly, "I . . . I need the job."

Jim shrugged. "What's going on at camp?"

"Nothing. They're just waiting around for

Mr. Saint to show up with the new construction boss."

Jim nodded. The waiter brought their food and they ate in silence for a while.

Paul Saint appeared in the doorway to the dining room. He searched the tables until he saw them and walked in to join them. Paul was dressed for traveling, a heavy wool jacket over whipcord britches tucked into polished boots. The jacket made him look bulkier than he was.

Jim kicked a chair out for him and Paul sat down.

Jim said, "Where's your sister, Mr. Saint?"

"At home," Paul answered shortly. "She's indisposed."

Jim frowned. "She appeared quite well last night."

Paul shrugged it off. "You know how women are—well one day, sick the next."

Dick looked up from his coffee, worry showing in his eyes. "I hope it's nothing serious, Mr. Saint?"

Paul looked coldly at him. "I don't believe it is." He added, "I don't remember asking you to come to town."

Dick flushed. "I . . ." He looked at Jim for help.

Jim brushed through his confusion. "We're about through here. Have you had your breakfast, Mr. Saint?"

"Never eat it," Paul answered. "Had coffee

at home." He got to his feet. "It's a long ride to camp. And I want to get back before night."

They rose. Jim paid the check for his and Dick's breakfasts and they went outside.

Paul climbed into the seat of his rented buggy and waited as Dick and Jim went to the stable for their mounts.

They rode out of town together.

From the window of the third floor of the hotel Donovan watched them, a cigar in his mouth. He waited until they were gone, then he went downstairs to breakfast. He had put pressure on Trans-Pecos' new construction boss and he had until tomorrow night before he turned to other means.

Trans-Pecos' main work camp lay along the creek, its wagons and teams staked out in rude shelters behind the workmen's tents. There were two long, hastily constructed frame buildings. One was a storeshed for tools and wire, the other was a galley.

One of the bigger tents had a board sign nailed to the cross timber above the flap door: OFFICE.

A single strand of wire ran from the telegraph pole set up just behind this tent and it afforded a direct connection with Paul Saint in town.

A half dozen men in wool shirts and trousers were grouped around an open fire when Paul

Saint, flanked by Dick and Jim Davis, rode into camp.

Dick continued on toward the horse sheds in back, but Paul and Jim pulled up a few yards away from the grouped men who had come to their feet, looking surprised and a little uncomfortable at Paul's visit.

Jack Sanders moved out to meet them. He was a stocky man in his forties with too much good nature showing in his blue eyes. He shook hands with Paul and looked at Jim, who had dismounted.

Paul said, "This is your new foreman, Jack. Walter Evans."

Jack's eyes showed a momentary surprise. Then he put out his hand and Jim shook it.

Jack said blandly, "We've been waiting for you, Mr. Evans. But—you surprise me." His blue eyes had a searching look. "Somehow I expected an older man."

Paul cut through this with brusque coldness. "How are things up here?"

Jack shrugged. "We're stalled." He nodded to Jim. "We were waiting for orders."

Jim looked around the camp. A stack of twenty foot fir poles, branches trimmed but with bark still in place, caught his eyes.

He said sharply, "You've got wire?"

Jack nodded. "In the storeshed."

"What's holding up the work?"

Jack flushed. "We're waiting on a new shipment of poles. Isn't enough in camp for more than a day's work."

"That would be one day closer to Fort Cochise, Mr. Sanders!" Jim's voice was brittle. He turned to Paul. "Where do we get our poles?"

"From Kingston Lumber Company—by rail." Paul studied Jim. "We've got a backlog stacked up behind the warehouse in town. Enough for a week's work."

Jim said, "See that they get here, Mr. Saint."

Paul's eyes held a small gleam. "I intended to, Mr. Evans." He looked at Jack, who was eyeing Jim, half in anger and surprise.

"Mr. Evans is in charge here. Any of you who feel you can't work for him can draw your time at my office."

"I don't think that will be necessary, Mr. Saint." Jim looked at the men behind Sanders. "I think we'll get along."

Paul shrugged. "Well, I have to get back." He climbed into the buggy, picked up his reins. "I'll see that you get your poles. And anything else you might need." He indicated the office tent. "You can keep in touch by wire. No need for you to come to town."

Jim nodded, watched him drive off.

He turned back to Sanders. The stocky man wasn't used to being pushed, and a small confusion showed in his eyes.

"Mr. Evans—" he began.

Jim cut him off. "Where's your telegrapher?"

"Out checking a break in the line." Jack frowned. "We tried to contact the office this morning, but the line was dead."

"You have that trouble often?" Jim's voice was hard.

Jack shrugged. "Only recently." He made a small gesture indicating he didn't think it was serious. "Not unusual, with the weather we've been having. Could be anything from a loose connection, pole down, erosion—"

"Not if it's done right in the first place!" Jim snapped. He put his attention to the men around the fire. But his question was fired at Jack. "Is this all of your crew?"

Jack retreated into puzzled anger. "Four men are at Shawlee's Slide, trying to save what's left of that pole shipment. The rest are here and in the tents."

"Get them out," Jim ordered. "I want to talk to them."

Jack turned to one of the men by the fire. "Harry—get the rest of the boys out here." He turned to Jim.

"We've got a good crew, Mr. Evans—as good as any in the business. But we can't do the impossible."

Jim moved toward the fire, picked up a tin cup, found the coffeepot, and poured himself a cup. The others eyed him, showing neither friendliness nor warmth.

Jim addressed them. "As you heard, I'm your new construction foreman. My job is to get this line through to Fort Cochise before the end of October. That means we start working right now, from sunup to dark, seven days a week!"

Jack said, "As long as we get paid, we'll work. But we've lost too much time, Mr. Evans."

Jim looked at him.

"I don't know how much you've been told," Jack added. "But with a fifty mile detour on top of all the delays—"

Jim cut him off. "We're going through Frenchy's Canyon, Mr. Sanders!"

Jack shook his head, but fell silent. Behind him Harry and four other men were coming up to the fire. One of them had a bad cold—he kept sneezing violently.

The men around the fire shifted uneasily. Burleson, a powerfully built man, shook his head. "I ain't working in that canyon, Mr. Evans." He seemed to be speaking for all of them.

"We have to," Jim said grimly. "There's only one way left to build this line on schedule: to work a twenty-four hour shift and go through that canyon. Any long detour and we might as well quit right here."

Burleson shook his head. "Not for me." He

58

looked at the others. "The rest of you are crazy if you do."

He started toward the tents.

Jim said, "Where are you going?"

Burleson looked back over his shoulder. "Get my things. I'm going into town and draw my time."

"We're paying double wages for overtime and a bonus to every man when the line is completed. I have Mr. Simpson's word on this."

Burleson hesitated. "Money isn't any good to a dead man."

Jim studied him. "You afraid of a fight?"

Burleson reacted. "Not with anything I can see. But that canyon—"

"I heard all about it," Jim snapped. "I don't know how Bill Davis and Orville died. That's one of the things I intend to find out." He let his gaze travel over that small group of men. "Sure, you'll have trouble. But not from ghosts." He let the silence sink in for a moment. In the background Dick Rainer was walking toward them.

"Any of you ever work for Overland?"

The rawboned man next to Burleson nodded.

"You know a man named Donovan?"

The man touched his flattened nose. "Used to be a line boss for Overland when they were building through to Fort Smith."

"I saw Donovan in town," Jim said. "He told me we didn't have a crew with the guts to ram this line through on schedule. Is he right?"

The men looked at one another. Most of them were old hands at stringing wire and they had a professional pride in their work.

Burleson spoke for them when he said, "We're not afraid of Donovan. But I know him. Overland has the money to hire killers. And we're not gunfighters."

"I don't expect you to be," Jim said grimly. "That's my job." He walked back to his horse, took his gun and belt from his saddle bag, buckled it on. He turned to Sanders.

"You handle the job here. I'll head off trouble."

Sanders looked dubious. "Donovan will bring in fast guns, Evans."

Jim studied the older man for a moment. The others were watching him. From a branch in the tree forty yards behind Jim a squirrel scolded.

Jim whirled and drew and fired all in one fast fluid motion. The squirrel tumbled off the branch, lay still.

Jim replaced the spent shell, shoved the gun back into his holster.

There was a long moment of silence. Then Jack said slowly, "Walter Evans was a good construction man . . . but he was a drunk when I knew him, ten years ago!" He looked at Jim, his voice hardening. "Who are you?"

Jim shrugged. "Some day I'll tell you." He eyed the men around Sanders. "That's my job—

handling trouble from Overland. Now get those wagons loaded and start stringing wire!"

He walked back to his horse and mounted. "I'm checking out Frenchy's Canyon. I expect to be back before dark—and I want to see a day's work done when I get back!"

He rode off, out of camp. Jack Sanders watched him for a long moment, then a tight smile broke the line of his lips. Someone else was taking over and he was a good second man.

"You heard him," he growled. "Let's get those wagons loaded. We're stringing wire!"

VIII

Mike Donovan had a leisurely breakfast and then walked slowly to the Trans-Pecos office. Only the telegrapher was behind the desk. He looked up as Mike approached.

Mike filled out a message blank and handed it to the man who read it back to him: "Harry Walton, c/o Shannon Hotel, King City. Send supplies we discussed. Mike."

He watched Mike leave and then turned to the telegraph key to send the wire. . . .

Mike paused outside to light a cigar. Then he walked leisurely to Sheriff Collins' office, a big man seemingly without a business care in the world.

The sheriff was not in, but his deputy, a lanky, hard-nosed man named Hank, was filling out a report. He was a poor hand with a pencil and this sort of work came hard for him.

Mike said, "Nice morning." He sounded pleasant enough. "Where's the sheriff?"

"Home. Weather's been bothering him." Hank eyed Mike impatiently. "Something I can do for you?"

Mike kept his temper with the young man, but it was an effort. Time enough to let go later.

"I was expecting a business associate on yesterday's train. I'm worried something may have happened to him." He shrugged. "Thought the sheriff might know something—"

Hank cut him off. "We don't keep a check of passengers, mister."

Mike shrugged. "Thanks, anyway," he said casually. He started to leave.

Hank said, "Wait." He studied the sheet in front of him for a moment, then stood up and took his hat. "We've got two dead men in the morgue. Maybe your friend is one of them."

They went out to the funeral parlor. Donovan looked at Evans' corpse.

"This your man?" Hank asked.

Donovan shook his head. "But I think I know who he is," he said slowly.

"I'm filling out an identification report," Hank said. "Come back to the office and—"

Donovan smiled. "I said I *think* I know who he is. I didn't say I was sure."

Hank studied him, annoyance crossing his features. "You either do or you don't," he said coldly.

"I'll know by tonight," Donovan answered. He walked out, leaving Hank staring after him . . .

Ellen Saint slept late and came to the office feeling out of sorts. She walked slowly to her desk, feeling the walls close in around her. Not that she minded the book work . . . it gave her

63

something to do; otherwise time would have dragged miserably for her.

But she was here because Paul had brought her, and she chafed at the restrictions imposed on her. Still, she had made her decision, a long time ago—money against the dubious opportunity for a career as an entertainer. It had turned bitter in her mouth, but she had no other place to go now.

She was at the filing cabinet when Donovan came into the office. He bowed politely as she turned to him.

"Miss Saint," he said, introducing himself, "I'm Mike Donovan of Overland."

Ellen looked him over. "My brother isn't here," she said. "He had to go out of town."

He nodded. "I know. Will you ask him to call on me. I'm staying at the hotel."

She frowned. "Does he know you, Mr. Donovan?"

"I'm sure he does," Mike said. "Tell him it's concerning his new construction boss, Walter Evans."

He turned away before she could ask him any questions.

Paul Saint arrived back in town in the afternoon and drove directly home for a change of clothes.

Ellen was in the office when he walked in. He

didn't give her a glance. He called the telegrapher over and said sharply, "Get Pop Stein in here right away."

The telegrapher disappeared into the warehouse in back of the office.

Ellen walked over to him as he stood by his desk, looking out across the room, his thoughts turned inward. She said, "Paul . . ." and then a little louder as he seemed not to notice her, "Paul . . . I'm sorry about last night."

He turned slowly to her, his thoughts still somewhere else. She put her hand on his arm . . . once she had been in love with this man and some old tentacle of that feeling stirred in her now. "Maybe it's just being here . . . in this small ugly town with no place to go—"

He shook her arm free. "I told you why we're here," he said coldly. "Until it's over, we'll both have to make the best of it."

The rebuff took the softness from Ellen's eyes. She started to turn away, then remembered Donovan.

"There's a man waiting for you at the hotel," she said curtly.

Paul looked at her, frowning.

"He said his name was Mike Donovan. He said you'd know him."

Paul nodded. "Did he say what he wanted?"

"He wants to talk to you—about Walter Evans."

Paul was silent for a moment. The telegrapher

came back into the office with Pop Stein, the warehouse foreman.

"How many wagons we got in the yard?" Paul asked.

"Two," Pop said. "One in the barn with a broken axle."

"Load them!" Paul snapped. "I want all those poles we've got stacked up ready to go first thing in the morning. I want them delivered to Cottonwood camp by tomorrow afternoon."

"Yes, sir," Stein said. He went back inside the warehouse. Paul turned to Ellen. "I'll see what Donovan has to say," he said.

"Paul—be careful!" A small worry showed in Ellen's eyes. "He was very polite—but I don't trust him."

"Neither do I," Paul answered. His smile was brittle. "But sometimes it helps to get a look at the other man's hole card. . . ."

Mike Donovan opened the door to Paul's knock. He was in shirtsleeves and smoking a thick cigar. The air in the room behind him was heavy with cigar smoke.

Two men were in the room with Donovan. They were in town clothes, but their coats barely concealed their holsters. They were quiet and respectable looking. Donovan didn't introduce them.

Donovan walked to a side table which held

glasses and a couple of bottles of bonded whiskey. He poured a drink for Paul and refilled his glass. The other two men already were holding their glasses.

He handed the drink to Paul. "Cheers," he said, smiling. It was the smile of a man holding the upper hand.

Paul said, "What do you want, Donovan?"

Mike shrugged. "Aw, come on now—you know me well enough to call me Mike." He lifted his glass again. "Let's drink to a reunion."

Paul watched him for a moment, then took a sip from his glass. He said coldly, "You wanted to talk to me about my construction foreman, Walter Evans?"

Mike grinned. "Your new construction foreman, yes. Not Walter Evans."

Paul frowned. Mike chuckled.

"Aw, come on now, Paul—you know he isn't Evans."

Paul's voice was stiff. "He had a letter from Mr. Simpson. Why wouldn't I believe he is Evans?"

"Because you had Evans killed," Mike said pleasantly.

Paul stood staring, his eyes narrowed.

"You don't have to look at me like that," Mike said. "I can't prove it—yet."

Paul put his glass down on the table. "I see I wasted my time coming here," he said coldly. He started for the door.

One of the men rose from his chair and moved to head him off. Paul paused, looking at Donovan.

Mike waved the man back.

"Evans' body is in the morgue," Mike said. The levity was gone from his voice now. It was hard, direct. "Walt used to work for Overland. I know him. I can identify him to the sheriff." He frowned. "What I want to know is who is the man who claims to be Evans?"

Paul took in a low breath. "I don't know."

Donovan stood a moment, lips pursed, eyes narrowed. Paul interjected; "I've got to get back to the office—"

"One more minute won't hurt you," Donovan cut in. As Paul looked at him, he said, "I've got a proposition to make to you."

Paul raised his shoulders in a slight shrug of indifference. But he waited.

Donovan turned to the two men and nodded toward the door. They rose and went out, closing the door behind them.

Donovan poured whiskey into Paul's glass then into his own. He raised his glass, downed it neat.

"I know you've sold out to Western. I want you to throw in with me." He cut off Paul's slight head shake. "Trans-Pecos isn't going to make it, Paul. Overland will take over completion of the line. You'll be out of a job. Give me a free hand

68

now to make sure Trans-Pecos folds. I don't want Western to get it."

Paul's lips tightened. There was a small gleam in his eyes. "I don't know what you're talking about, Mike. I'm working for Trans-Pecos—"

"Like hell you are!" Donovan shot at him. "You've sold out to Western. That's why Trans-Pecos is behind schedule now. I just want to make sure Overland is in position to take over when Trans-Pecos folds."

Paul's smile was enigmatic. "What are you offering?"

"Branch manager with the new line, and a substantial sum of money. At least as much as Western promised you."

"No."

Donovan's eyes turned flinty. "All right, Paul. We could have worked this together. But we're going to break Trans-Pecos and take over—and you'll be cut out of it!"

Paul shrugged. "Maybe," he said softly. "Maybe not." He put his untouched glass down on the table and walked out.

Donovan stood looking at the closed door for a long moment. Compromise had never been his strong point. But he had been under orders to effect a deal with Paul Saint, if he could. If not—?

Now a small and wicked smile touched his lips. He had tried. He didn't know why Paul Saint had refused. But he did know that he now had a free hand to stop Trans-Pecos in the ways he knew best.

He picked up Paul's glass. No sense to waste good whiskey. He finished it and laid the glass down.

That was one thing about Overland, he reflected—the men running it were out to win. By merger, financial manipulation, political intrigue—even bribery. But sometimes it came down to fundamentals, to a rough and tumble fight between men. And in this area Mike Donovan felt at home.

He went down to the bar where his two men were sitting at a corner table, playing pinochle. He nodded only casually as he went on through to the dining room.

The two men quit playing. They moved on to the lobby, and went out.

Donovan didn't look back. Tomorrow, or the day after, the others would be coming into town, in reply to his telegram.

Trans-Pecos was finished, anyhow. But a man needed a good fight to keep from getting flabby, and he hadn't been in one in a long time.

He wondered just how much of a fight the man who called himself Walter Evans would put up.

IX

The wind whistled forlornly through the gutted and decaying windows of the old house as Jim pulled up in the yard beside the stone-rimmed well. The thick hemp rope coiled around the windlass was weathered and rotted, but it still preserved an appearance of efficiency, its end knotted about the handle of the oak bucket dangling over the well.

The fire had gutted only the main house: it had left untouched the big barn, the corrals, the tool shed. But these, like the well, were bowing to time and weather, sagging a bit tiredly, like a proud man grown old and giving in to the years reluctantly.

Jim studied the house for a moment. Through the blackened, skeletal framework he could see the remains of what had been a curving stairway, in the grand manner, rising into the nothingness above. . . .

A man could, if he was inclined that way, hear the ghostly mutter of Frenchy and his young wife, quarreling . . . one could hear anything his mind imagined, Jim thought, but the wind did not explain his brother's death, nor that of his companion, Steve Orville.

He stepped down from the saddle and walked

71

toward the house. A ground squirrel scurried from under a shapeless mound of blackened boards and disappeared into a hole in a cutbank beyond. Jim looked down at the gun which reflex had put in his hand; he smiled wryly and slid it back into holster.

He cut around to the back of the house and studied the cliff which rose steeply less than a quarter of a mile away. It was a natural place for a ranch, the high cliffs protecting it from the northern winds. But, given more time, no man would have chosen to string wire through this canyon. Bill Davis had been forced by a tight schedule to this alternate route and Jim knew there was no other way for Trans-Pecos to go.

He studied the cliff, knowing they would have to string the wire from base to crest, thereby increasing the possibility of line breakage due to chafing. And a break anywhere along the five hundred foot ascent would be hard to repair quickly.

Beyond that crest lay another hundred miles of rough, practically deserted country. Jim faced the prospect that he would have to split his work crew into two detachments—one working from the Cottonwood Creek camp to the base of this cliff, the other, with the remaining wagons and team of horses, cutting around and through Quartzite Pass and then doubling back to the top of the cliff.

To save time they would have to freight poles, wire and insulators to this point and then hoist them by hand winch and pulley to the crew on top.

And the thought came to him that a hundred things could go wrong before they reached Fort Cochise—an early snowstorm, a premature freeze, accidents, sickness—and Donovan's guns. In a way it was like a giant roulette wheel with a countless number of possibilities. He shrugged off the thought and remembered his brother. Bill's death was tied up with Trans-Pecos and so, in a way, was he.

Behind him his horse whinnied. He turned quickly, his gaze moving downcanyon. He saw nothing, but the feeling persisted that he was being watched.

He mounted and rode back toward camp.

Clouds began to pile up against the distant horizon. Blue-black, they looked cold. Unconsciously Jim rubbed his hands together.

The old wagon road curved ahead of him, moving in close to the canyon side. Above it, on a shelf of rock, he saw the old miner's shack . . . it seemed to hang out over the road, desolate and unoccupied.

On impulse Jim dismounted and scrambled up the slope to the cabin. A few yards behind it the black mouth of a mine tunnel gaped at him; its bracing timbers sagged dangerously.

Jim eyed it for a moment, then went inside the cabin. It was devoid of any furniture it might have had, its earthen floor bounded by four timbered walls.

Jim crossed to the glassless window and crouched down as something caught his eye. He picked up the charred remnants of a wood match, then studied the earthen floor. He could make out faint boot prints. A man had stood here, looking out on the canyon road below. Not recently, but not too long ago, either.

He stood up. Through the paneless window he could look down on the old road and he saw that riders coming back from the gutted remains of Frenchy's place would have to pass within twenty feet of this window.

His brother and Steve Orville would have passed this way. But whoever killed them had not used a gun.

He went back to his horse and mounted and rode away. Behind him the cold wind rose and it seemed to make a sound of gibberish laughter behind him.

Jack Sanders rubbed his cold hands together and turned his back on the biting wind. The posthole diggers had finished their work and gone back to the Cottonwood Creek camp. This was the last of the poles being erected, the terminus of the Trans-Pecos line . . . for the time being, at least.

He watched as lines were attached to the twenty-five foot pole. Burleson, holding one end of the thick rope coiled around the base of the pole, leaned back as the driver of the team flicked his animals forward.

The butt end of the pole, guided by the straining Burleson, slid into the posthole, scraping a furrow into the side as the horses, moving forward, brought the pole slowly upright. It slid into place and was immediately shored up by the timber men, using long pole rods. The crew worked swiftly, tamping the earth firmly into place, buttressing the cedar pole and firming it with heavy rocks around its base.

A ladder was set into place against the pole and a man went up to hammer an insulator into place a foot below the pole's crown.

Jack motioned to the wire stringers coming up behind. The line of poles already erected made their stand behind them, diminishing in their backward march to camp.

The wire man went up the ladder and secured the wire from the big reel on the wagon. He wound it once around the insulator and waved a *go ahead* to the man driving.

The team moved forward, slowly, and the slack in the wire was taken up. It came up off the ground between the last pole and the one on which the wire man waited, tightening slowly. The insulator man held up a hand . . . the team stopped.

Jack called, "Make sure she's tight, Lou," and the man on the ladder nodded. He put a gloved hand on the taut iron wire, tested it, he made a short motion to the driver and the man touched a light rein on the back of his team. The horses edged slightly forward. Now the wind thrummed along the wire, making a peculiar, desolate sound.

The man on the ladder judged the tautness of the wire as much by the sound it made as by its feel. He drove in the holding nails on the insulator, pinning the wire between the glass ridges, and came down the ladder.

Jack said, "We'll have to leave the rest of the wire here until we get a new shipment of poles—" then he turned as a rider came into sight around a bend in the barely discernible old road they had been following.

Davis rode up and eyed the poles. Jack walked up to him. "Last of the poles," he said shortly. "I sent the diggers back to camp."

Jim nodded. He looked around, saw several new faces.

Jack motioned one of the new men over, a ruddy-faced, stocky man, in the middle thirties. "Our new construction boss—" He hesitated a moment, then added, "Mr. Evans."

The new man nodded acknowledgment. "This is Charley Murdock," Jack said to Davis. "He salvaged some of the poles that went down into Shawlee's Slide."

Murdock frowned. "Couldn't tell if it was an accident or not, Mr. Evans. That bridge was temporary, but it held all right for us before." He took a breath. "Morgan, the driver, was killed. I sent a couple of the men into town with the body."

Jim nodded. He looked at Sanders. "Where's his family?"

Sanders shrugged. "Somewhere back East. Mr. Saint has their address." He rubbed his cold hands together. "Not much more we can do, until we get a new shipment of poles."

"We can dig postholes!" Davis said sharply. "I want a crew out at dawn . . . I want them digging postholes from here to the base of the cliffs behind Frenchy's burned-out place."

"We're going through the canyon, Mr. Evans?" Murdock asked.

Jim nodded. He looked at Sanders. "We do have a right-of-way—an easement?"

Sanders frowned. "Must have. Bill Davis would never have decided to go through without it." He turned to Murdock. "You remember anything about it, Charley?"

"Steve Orville made the arrangements," Murdock answered. "Cleared it with some relative living in New Orleans. I think Mr. Saint has the paper in his office."

"I'll check on it," Jim said. "And on those poles, too."

He swung around and saw Dick Rainer by the wire wagon and motioned him over.

"Ever handle a rifle before?" Jim asked the boy.

"I've done a little hunting," Dick answered.

Jim slid his rifle from his saddle scabbard, tossed it to him. He found a box of shells in his saddlebags and handed it over too.

"I want you to stand by the diggers."

Dick flushed. "Yes, sir, Mr. Evans!"

Jim turned to the others. "With Donovan in town, we'll have to expect trouble. I'm going to pick up rifles, shotguns and shells. Donovan told me we weren't going to finish this line. I told him he was wrong."

Jim paused, looking at the men.

"Seems like we're not only going to have to beat a tight schedule, we're going to have to fight!" He waited a moment. "Anyone want to ride to town with me and draw his time?"

No one moved.

Jack said grimly, "Get those posts to us, Mr. Evans . . . we'll get them up!"

Jim smiled. He turned and rode away.

X

Doctor Sawyer said good night to the tired middle-aged woman for whom he could do little but smile and prescribe a tonic. He knew and she knew that the gnawing pain inside her was incurable, but she didn't complain and he had nothing else to offer her.

When she had gone he walked to the window and looked out into the night, a thin sharp-nosed man, old and gray and shabby, hiding his incompetence behind a brisk, truculent manner.

His reflection on the dirty window panes blurred whatever he could see outside, but the cold wet street offered him nothing he had not seen a hundred times. He did not feel depressed—he did not feel anything. He had lived all of his life in towns like this.

A long time ago he had studied medicine, apprenticing out to a doctor in Oklahoma City, and then he'd come west to hang out his shingle in Junction City. He knew how to treat a bullet wound, but there were butchers who could take out a lead slug with less mess.

It was not that he had not wanted to do better. But he lacked drive and he hadn't really cared to put in the necessary time and sweat to learn his trade. His wife had left him several years ago, taking their daughter with her, and had gone back home. . . . He now lived as he pleased and didn't really miss them.

The knock on his front door intruded on his moment of quiet. He frowned, wondering whom it might be. It was too cold to go out on a call, and things had been relatively quiet in town—he had heard of no recent trouble that might require his services.

He went into the front room and took a worn volume of *Gray's Anatomy* from his meager shelf and opened it at random, setting it down on the table so that whoever was at the door would get the impression he had interrupted the doctor at his reading.

When he opened the door the face staring at him was strange to Dr. Sawyer. He frowned slightly, waiting for the man to speak.

Jim Davis said, "I'd like a word with you, Doctor."

Sawyer eyed the young-hard face, the coldly searching gray eyes. He said, "It is after my office hours. If it isn't urgent—"

"It is, to me," Davis said. He looked past Sawyer, into the room. "If you're busy, I'll wait."

Sawyer shrugged, waved Jim inside. He closed the door behind him.

"What can I do for you, Mr. . . . ?"

"Jim Davis," Jim said. "I'm the new construction foreman for Trans-Pecos."

"Oh!" Sawyer took his steel-rimmed spectacles from his pocket, put them on. He was groping for recognition, but the name had not yet made a connection in his mind.

"What's your trouble, Mr. Davis?"

"I want to know how my brother died."

Sawyer stared at Jim for a moment. "Your brother—?" Then, remembering: "Of course— Bill Davis. Former construction boss for Trans-Pecos."

Jim nodded.

Sawyer shrugged. "It's in my medical report, Mr. Davis."

"I haven't read it."

Sawyer turned. "I'll get it for you."

"You don't have to," Jim interrupted. "Just tell me."

Sawyer said, "I don't know if I should." His tone was truculent. "Trans-Pecos didn't believe in my capability. They sent for a doctor from Denver."

This was new to Jim.

"An autopsy?"

Sawyer nodded. "Mr. Saint has the report in his office. A copy of mine, too." Sawyer made a gesture of dissatisfaction. "The company could have saved itself the money. Essentially, they diagnosed your brother's death the same as I did."

"How did my brother and Steve Orville die?"

"Just stopped breathing."

Jim's eyes narrowed angrily and Dr. Sawyer added quickly, "That's about it, Mr. Davis. I examined both your brother and Steve Orville. Not a mark on them. But—they definitely died of asphyxiation."

"Poisoned?"

"I don't think so." Sawyer thought for a moment. "Whatever it was, it killed quickly. If it was something they had taken at breakfast, they would not have had time to leave camp." He made a small gesture of helplessness. "Of course, I have read somewhere of drugs or chemicals that could cause this type of death. However, they are not common . . . and I could not, at this moment, even tell you what they are."

Jim nodded. "Thanks, anyway, Doctor." He turned to leave, paused. "I got news of my brother's death late. I know he was buried here—"

"Cemetery behind the church . . . part way up the hill."

Sawyer walked to the door with Jim and watched him mount and ride away.

The cemetery was enclosed by a low stone wall and Junction City had been in existence long enough for a sizable number of its inhabitants to come to rest here.

It appeared to Jim, as he paused just inside the rusted iron gate, that the more affluent had chosen the northeast corner of the cemetery for their own, the survivors erecting markers and crosses of stone, some of massive and ostentatious size, perhaps reflecting an oblique effort at some sort of atonement for neglect or anger during the life of the deceased.

The southeast corner was more cramped with small wooden markers. In between, his brother and Steve Orville were buried. Trans-Pecos had footed the expense, which included a small stone headboard, chiseled into the gray slab was Bill's name, his date of birth and the time of his death and nothing more.

Jim walked up to Bill's grave and looked down. Some freshly cut flowers in a clay pot gave a touch of color and remembrance to the otherwise bleak scene. The same flowers and pot rested on Orville's grave, and Jim guessed that the flowers were from the Orville family, for Bill had never married and he could think of no one in Junction City who would go to the trouble.

Jim looked down at his brother's grave for a long moment. He remembered now the small things a man remembers about his brother when they had been boys, growing up on a small farm in Ohio . . . things of no importance to anyone but Jim and which he knew were gone forever.

The sound of a carriage driving up behind him

intruded upon his thoughts, but Jim did not turn around until he heard footsteps on the soggy path behind him.

The two men coming toward him wore badges. They were shadowy figures in the dark and didn't take definite form until they were within a few feet of Jim. Then Jim saw that one was paunchy and graying; he looked unhappy at coming out on a night like this. The man with him was twenty years younger, tall, thin and morose.

The paunchy man said mildly, "I'm Sheriff Collins. My deputy, Hank."

Jim Davis nodded slightly and let his gaze go to the man waiting in the buggy just outside the cemetery wall. He could not make out the man's features, but the heavy, solid shape suggested Mike Donovan.

"Something we can do for you?" the sheriff asked. His voice sounded tired, and there was a touch of misery in it.

"Nothing I can think of," Jim said evenly.

Collins sighed. "Then perhaps you can do something for us." He acted like a man who had come to this unwillingly. "We'd like to ask you a few questions, Mr. Evans."

Jim shrugged. "This is hardly the place—"

Hank drew his gun.

Jim's smile was cold. "Anything you say, sheriff."

"You are Walter Evans?"

84

Jim glanced to the dark bulk of Donovan waiting in the carriage. He regretted now that he had taken Evans' name when he had checked in with Paul Saint, but it had seemed like a good idea at the time.

"No," he said quietly to the sheriff's question.

Sheriff Collins frowned. "But you registered at the hotel as Walter Evans?"

Jim nodded.

"I understand that you represented yourself to Mr. Paul Saint as Walter Evans, also?"

Jim didn't say anything.

Hank said coldly, "Who are you?"

Jim shrugged. "Mr. Saint knows who I am."

Collins looked at his deputy. It was plain that the matter rested in Hank's hands.

"Does he?" Hank's tone was skeptical. He made a motion with his gun. "Let's check with Mr. Saint and find out, shall we?"

Paul Saint opened his door and looked surprised at the men waiting.

Jim said, "Sorry to bother you after hours, Mr. Saint. But I seem to have run into some trouble with the law."

Paul's glance moved to Donovan standing behind the sheriff. The big man smiled thinly.

Paul's features gave no hint of what he was thinking. "Come in, gentlemen."

They went inside.

The sheriff walked directly to the log fire, turning his back to it. He was not comfortable here. Paul Saint represented Trans-Pecos, and the wire company was a political power in the state. But then, so was Donovan. Collins didn't like the feeling of being in the middle of a power struggle.

Mike Donovan glanced cursorily around the small living room. He was only mildly interested in the trophies gracing the walls.

"I'm sure you can clear this up for us, Paul," the sheriff said.

He turned and took off his hat as Ellen appeared on the staircase. She paused, a small surprise in her eyes, then continued on down into the living room.

"Nice of you to stop by," she said graciously. "Can I get you and your friends something to warm you?"

Collins shook his head. "We won't be but a few minutes." He turned back to Paul, hesitated, then indicated Jim Davis. "This new construction boss of yours—you know who he is?"

Paul's glance went from Jim to Mike Donovan. The big Overland boss was waiting, a thin smile in his eyes.

Paul shrugged. "Of course."

Collins frowned. "Is he Walter Evans?"

Paul said, "No." He was watching Donovan, a small sardonic light in his eyes. "Walter Evans is dead, isn't he, Vic? Mike must have told you. He knew Evans."

Vic Collins looked confused.

Donovan's teeth clamped hard on his cigar. "I knew Walter Evans," he said. "But I wasn't sure you did."

Hank said curtly, "Then who is *this* man, Paul?"

Paul turned to face Jim, a small light dancing in his eyes. "Maybe you'd better tell them," he said.

Admiration for Paul Saint's unruffled handling of the situation glinted briefly in Jim's eyes.

He nodded. "I'm Jim Davis," he said. "Bill Davis was my brother. Mr. Simpson hired me. You can verify it by wire."

Only the barest flicker of surprise showed in Paul Saint's eyes. He turned to the sheriff. "What's the problem, Vic?"

Collins shook his head. His bones ached and he wanted to get back into bed.

"Nothing, long as you know who he is, Paul." He turned to Donovan. "Are you satisfied?"

Donovan's teeth showed in a cold smile. He had been outfoxed by Paul Saint, and he knew it. "I'm satisfied—if Mr. Saint is."

Collins turned to go, but Hank stopped him. "Maybe Mr. Donovan is satisfied, Vic. But I'm not." He looked at Jim, an angry light in his eyes.

"You signed in at the hotel as Walter Evans. You must have known Evans was dead!"

"I knew," Jim said quietly. He took Evans' letter of introduction from his pocket and handed it to the deputy. "I found Evans' body about a hundred yards from the railroad tracks. Someone shot him and pushed him off the train as it was coming into Junction City. I was on the trail, riding in."

Hank read the letter quickly, handed it to the sheriff. He looked at Saint. "You knew about this?"

Paul took a moment before answering. "Yes."

Hank's lips tightened. "You could have told us."

Paul turned to the sheriff, deliberately ignoring the deputy. "As you well know, Vic," he said coldly, "we're running behind schedule. I suggested that Davis take Evans' place until Mr. Simpson could hire another construction foreman."

Collins handed the letter back to Jim. "You didn't see who killed Evans?"

"No."

Hank's anger was barely controllable. "Nice of you to let us in on your arrangements, Mr. Saint." His lips curled. "You'll take care of the body, of course?"

Paul nodded. "As soon as I hear from Mr. Simpson." His tone was cold. "Now if you'll excuse us, sheriff? I have to get to the office early in the morning."

Hank started to say something, but Collins

stopped him. Elections were coming up next month and Collins didn't want to antagonize Paul Saint.

He turned to Ellen. "Sorry if we disturbed you, Miss Saint."

"Not at all." Ellen smiled graciously.

She walked with them to the door, then came back and looked at Jim Davis.

Paul motioned to the stairs. "Leave us, Ellen!"

Ellen didn't move. This night she was not going to be ordered around by Paul, and her eyes told him so.

Paul's tone hardened. "Go back to bed, Ellen!"

Ellen shook her head. "I want to hear what Mr. Davis has to say, Paul."

"Let her stay," Jim cut in. "This concerns all of us."

Paul hesitated. He did not like to be disobeyed by Ellen, but he could tend to her later. He turned to Jim, his eyes cold and narrowed.

"I saved your hide tonight, Davis! You know that, don't you?"

"You saved me from answering a lot of unpleasant questions," Jim said.

Paul studied him for a moment, then walked closer to the fireplace. His face was hard and unreadable in the flickering flame light.

"How do I know you didn't kill Walter Evans?"

"You'll have to take my word for it."

Paul's voice was cold. "I'll take your word only

when I hear from Mr. Simpson about you." He picked up his pipe from the small table near the big easy chair, but his hand trembled slightly. "I don't know why Warren Simpson hired you, or why you came here posing as Evans. But I'm still in charge of this line from Junction City. Either Simpson okays that, or I leave!"

His smile ran thin and cold on his lips. "And I don't think Trans-Pecos can stand my leaving, Davis!"

Jim's voice was mild. "I didn't come here to replace you."

"Why did you come?"

"I want the man who killed my brother."

Ellen started slightly. "Killed him?" She looked at Paul, her eyes dark and questioning.

"No one killed your brother," Paul said sharply. "I told you what happened. No one really knows how he died—"

"I do!" Jim's voice was even.

Paul stared at him for a long moment. "You know who killed him?"

"Not yet."

Paul brought a lighted match to his pipe. "I don't believe anyone killed your brother. But I understand how you feel." He tossed the burned-out match into the fireplace. "But chasing after a supposed killer isn't going to help Trans-Pecos, is it, Davis?"

Jim shrugged. "The wire comes first." His eyes

had a dark, brooding look for a moment. "Bill started on this job for Trans-Pecos—I want to finish it for him."

"You don't have time," Paul said harshly. He walked back to Jim. "And even if you could make it, there's Donovan—"

"I'll take care of Donovan!" Jim snapped.

"Maybe." Paul's lips twisted coldly. "Mike's got two gunmen standing by in town right now. And I know how he works. There's more on the way." He shook his head. "I don't know how good you are with a gun, Davis. But you can't fight Donovan and run a wire crew at the same time!"

"We're going to give it a try," Jim said. He walked to the door, looked back. "I'm going to need a dozen rifles. And shells."

Paul frowned. "For the crew?"

Jim nodded.

Paul didn't like the idea. "All you'll do is get some of the men killed. They're not gunmen."

"Get me the rifles," Jim said. "I'll worry about who gets killed."

Paul shrugged. "They'll be ready for you in the morning."

He watched Jim leave, then turned to Ellen. His eyes had an unpleasant look.

"Paul," she said, walking toward him, "let's leave now. Before he finds out—"

Paul slapped her.

She brought her hand up slowly to her cheek, the light in her eyes fading.

"We'll leave when Trans-Pecos folds," he said harshly. "That's why we came here, Ellen. To break Warren Simpson!"

Ellen turned and walked toward the stairs. She turned then to look with stony gaze at the man by the fire.

"Did you kill Bill Davis?"

He looked at her, not answering, his eyes steady on her, cruel as a jungle animal's.

"Because if you did," she said slowly, "I'm sorry for you." He only smiled and she turned and walked slowly up to her room and closed the door, then bolted it.

She lay across the bed and wanted to cry, but the tears wouldn't come. She wasn't crying for Paul. She wanted to cry for herself . . . for the four years she had lived with a man she thought she had loved.

XI

Sheriff Collins paused in front of the law office and looked at his deputy. They had walked in silence from Paul Saint's house and Vic sensed the quiet anger in the lanky man by his side.

"Lock up and go home," he said. His voice was tired. "You're not being paid to work twenty-four hours a day."

Hank shook his head.

Vic eyed him for a moment, then sighed. "All right—come out with it. What's bothering you?"

Hank did not feel like arguing. "Vic—I know you're not feeling well—"

Collins' tone hardened. "I don't feel that bad, Hank!"

Hank shrugged. "There's two dead men lying on slabs in Sam's back room. One of them is a construction boss for Trans-Pecos. He was shot. The other one, with the busted head—I think I've seen him around town. But—"

Vic cut in sharply. "Forget it, Hank!"

Hank stared at his boss. "Forget it? Like we did about Bill Davis and Steve Orville?"

"We did what we could," Vic said.

"Sure." Hank's voice held a sharp sarcasm. "We rode around a bit, nosed through Frenchy's Canyon, then came back and washed our hands—"

Collins' voice was rough. "What else could we do? We don't even know how they died."

"We know how Evans died!" Hank snapped.

Collins said nothing for a moment . . . he stared down the cold dark street with bitter eyes. Then he turned, put a hand on Hank's shoulder.

"Hank," he said slowly, "there's nothing we can do. Lock up and go home—"

Hank shook his head stubbornly. "We didn't have much to go on with Bill Davis and the others. But I think I've got a lead on who killed Evans. Just give me—"

"No!" Collins' voice was sharp. Then his tone softened. "Hank—this is between Trans-Pecos and Overland. You start nosing around and neither you nor I will be wearing a badge next month."

Hank was bitter. "What's a badge good for if you can't use it?"

Collins shivered as a cold wind made its run up the street. There was an ache in his bones and his eyes watered. *I am getting old,* he thought. There had been a time when he relished winter, the bite of an icy wind. There had been a time when, like Hank, he would not have been afraid to buck Trans-Pecos or Overland to uphold the law.

"Look," he said kindly. "Even if I said go ahead, you wouldn't get anywhere. Mike Donovan's in town, and he speaks for Overland. He knows Trans-Pecos is in trouble—he's waiting to pick up the pieces. It's not a new story—"

"That doesn't change things," Hank said. "Someone killed Walter Evans. If what you say about Overland is true, Donovan probably had a hand in it."

"Probably. But we'll never prove it." Collins shrugged. "They're too big for us, Hank. Even if we managed to get enough evidence to bring Donovan to court he'd never be convicted."

Hank said bitterly, "If you work for a big rich company you can get away with murder. Is that it, Vic?"

"I'm saying it's something you and I can't handle!" Collins was losing his temper. "I'm going to make a full report to the United States Marshal's office in the morning. They're federal. Let them handle it."

Hank was silent.

Vic sighed. "There are limitations to a county sheriff's authority, Hank. The sooner you realize it, the easier it'll go for you."

Hank took a long breath. "All right, Vic," he said sourly. "I'll keep my nose clean." His voice carried a thin sarcasm. "Where else can I draw wages for doing nothing?"

Collins eyed the bitter deputy for a long, troubled moment. He had come to like the man during their four years of association.

"Sleep on it," he said, managing a small smile. "I'll see you in the morning."

He turned and walked off.

Hank stood on the walk in front of the law office, thinking things over. He wasn't married and he wasn't sleepy, and he had nothing else he wanted to do.

He went inside, blew out the light, and locked the office. The lights of the Railroad Saloon flanking the hotel caught his attention and he made his way toward it.

There was a sprinkling of diehard customers inside. The three house girls stood around the piano, looking less than gay despite their spangled plumage. There would be no real action until the weekend and the weather was keeping things quieter than usual.

Hank crossed to the bar and unpinned his badge. He tossed it on the counter in front of the bartender, who stared at him.

"Keep this for me, Lou," Hank said. "And give me a bottle of that under-the-counter whiskey you keep for your best customers. I'm celebrating tonight."

Lou frowned. "Two's generally your limit, Hank. You sure you want the bottle?"

Hank nodded. He started to unbuckle his gun-belt as Lou placed a glass and a full bottle on the counter in front of him.

"Better keep this for me, too." Hank's smile had a bitter hardness. "I don't want to get into any trouble tonight."

He placed the loaded gunbelt on the counter, picked up the bottle and the glass.

He held up the bottle. "When this is finished, just help me to the door and point me toward the boardinghouse. Okay, Lou?"

Lou nodded.

He watched Hank make his way to an unoccupied table, then he shook his head, placed Hank's badge and gunbelt on the shelf under the counter and went on to serve another customer.

Mike Donovan opened the door of his hotel room and motioned to the two men waiting outside to come in.

"It's a cold night," he said. "One for the road."

They went in and Donovan closed the door behind them. He pointed to the whiskey bottle and glasses on the table. "Help yourselves."

Spade Larkin, a tall man with a small crescent scar over his left eye, glanced at his companion, Grady, who went to do the honors.

Donovan chewed thoughtfully on the end of his fat cigar. "You check out Frenchy's Canyon?"

Spade nodded. He and Grady were quiet men. Professionals. They had been with Donovan a long time. Donovan took care of all the labor troubles for Overland, and Spade and Grady worked with him.

"How's it stack up?"

Spade shrugged. "They've got an outside

chance of making it, going through that canyon. But they'll have to split their work force. And they'll have to string wire and haul their supplies up a five hundred foot cliff behind that burned-out ranchhouse."

Grady came back and handed Spade his glass. He looked at Donovan. "Who's the new Trans-Pecos construction boss?"

"Man named Jim Davis. Claims he's Bill Davis' brother." Donovan walked to the table, poured himself a drink. "Either of you know anything about him?"

Spade and Grady exchanged glances. Spade said quietly, "Should we have?"

Donovan took a swallow from his glass. "I thought you might. He's a gunman."

Spade's eyes brightened. "So Simpson finally hired himself a real troubleshooter?"

Donovan nodded.

Grady said, "He kill Walt Evans?"

"I don't think so," Donovan replied. "My guess is Paul Saint had Evans killed." He finished his drink, set his empty glass down. "Saint's been playing his own game. I think he's out to wreck Trans-Pecos for personal reasons. But with Davis on the scene, he'll have to toe the line."

Spade frowned. "Saint didn't come in with us, then?"

Donovan chuckled. "No. He thinks he's got us outsmarted. He's going to let us stop Trans-

Pecos for him." He shoved his cigar back into his mouth. "We'll let him think so."

Grady said, "They'll be a small advance work crew at the Canyon. What do you want, Mike?"

"You've done it before," Donovan said. "No killing, unless you have to."

"What about Davis?" Spade's question was casual.

"He's in town. You may have to kill him when he comes looking for you. But—" Donovan grinned—"I'll have a crack at him first." He held up a balled hand, its knuckles scarred from innumerable rough-and-tumble fights. "My way."

Spade smiled coldly. "A bullet finishes it quicker."

Donovan eyed the gunman. Spade had the cold, emotionless viewpoint of his kind. No unnecessary violence, no needless chances. A clean, quick job.

"Everybody to his own satisfactions," he said.

He walked to the door with them.

Spade said, "What about the law?"

"Sheriff Collins and his deputy will stay out of it. Anything else will be handled directly from the main office."

Spade nodded.

Grady asked, "When are the others due in?"

"On the morning train." Donovan looked at Larkin. "They're sending a new man with the old crew. Name's Petersen."

Spade looked at Grady. "Len Petersen?"

Donovan nodded. "You know him?"

"We heard of him."

Donovan studied his two men. "How fast is he with a gun?"

Spade took a moment before answering. "If he's as good as his reputation, I wouldn't want to cross him."

Donovan smiled. "Guess the main office really wants this line." He shrugged. "They've got an old score to settle with Warren Simpson . . . they're making sure this time."

Spade hesitated. "I don't know, Mike. Petersen's not a company man." There was a faint resentment in his tone. "We could have handled it."

"Just added insurance," Donovan said. "Don't worry about Petersen."

He closed the door behind them and walked slowly to the window. He felt restless, rusty . . . he hadn't gotten into a good fight in a long time.

He turned and walked back to the table and poured himself a drink.

Everything was efficiency these days: a half dozen hired strong arm boys to rough up the Trans-Pecos work crews; men like Spade, Grady and Petersen to handle any gun trouble.

In the old days it had been different. Overland was a small outfit, then, fighting for bids, taking its chances along with the half dozen rival wire companies. And a good construction boss had to first lick the ablest men in his crew before he gained the right to lead them.

Donovan set his glass down on the table. He wondered how much pushing a man like Jim Davis would take. Then he smiled broadly, rubbing his knuckles in anticipation.

It would be a pleasure to find out.

XII

The Orville house was like the others on the street, small but comfortable and set back from a small picket fence. Both the fence and the house had been recently painted and it appeared that the occupants had decided to stay in Junction City. But the small sign nailed to the fence to one side of the gate said: FOR SALE—INQUIRE WITHIN.

Jim Davis glanced at the sign as he opened the gate and walked to the front door. He had met Steve Orville briefly, years ago, but not Steve's family. Working for Trans-Pecos was an on the move job and Steve's wife, it seemed, was always in the process of catching up with him. It couldn't have been much of a life, Jim reflected, and now that aspect of it was over for her and he could understand her wanting to leave Junction City.

The girl who answered his knock was tall and pretty and young. Jim could make out this much in the darkness of the yard.

"Mrs. Orville?"

"My mother's inside," the girl said. "I'm Bess." She waited in the doorway.

"I'm the new construction boss for Trans-Pecos," Jim said. "I'd like to talk to your mother."

Bess hesitated. "We heard a new man was coming to take Bill Davis' place."

"I'm his brother," Jim said.

She stood still a moment, then said, "Please come in."

Jim followed her into the kitchen where Mrs. Orville, a little heavier than her daughter but still remarkably good-looking and only slightly graying, was packing some kitchen items into a box. She paused as they came inside and Bess said, "This is Bill Davis' brother, Mother. He wants to see you."

Mrs. Orville studied Jim briefly. She was dressed in black, and her blue eyes, direct and noncommittal, did not reflect the censure in her voice.

"You're late for the funeral," she said. "But I can show you where he is buried . . ."

"I've been there," Jim said.

"You come to pay your respects?"

"I've been given his job."

Mrs. Orville's eyes widened at this. "Well," she said, and then gave him a somewhat strained smile. "That's nice." She waved to a chair by the kitchen table. "Not that it matters now."

Jim looked at her, feeling the faint animosity in her and trying to understand it.

"Oh, sit down," she said heavily, and looking at Bess; added, "I'm sure Mr. Davis wouldn't mind some coffee. I'd like some, too."

Jim sat down and she settled in a chair across from him. "Don't mind the house," she said. "We're getting ready to move, as soon as we find a buyer."

Bess brought cups and saucers and set a place for herself. "We've got some milk, if you use it," she offered.

He shook his head and Bess poured the coffee.

"Your brother used to talk about you," Mrs. Orville said. "You've been out of the country, haven't you?"

He nodded. He noticed that Bess' eyes were on him, frankly wondering. He wondered what Bill had said about him.

"I've been moving around," he said quietly.

"You're not in trouble with the law?" the older woman asked sharply.

He smiled. "No."

She was silent for a moment. "I never knew your brother to carry a gun," she said. "My husband didn't, either." Her eyes were a little hard, and a little angry. "All they wanted to do was string wire for Trans-Pecos. Steve said that some day it would tie the country together."

She took a sip of her coffee and looked at Jim and shrugged. "You probably want to know how your brother died."

"I know how he died," Jim said quietly.

The older woman frowned. "Then you know more than the doctors who—"

104

"Curare," Jim said. "A quick-acting poison—from South America." He looked at Bess. "Usually smeared on the tip of a small dart and fired from a blowgun."

Mrs. Orville looked directly at him. "Then you're saying someone deliberately killed Bill and my husband?"

"Yes." His smile was small and cold. "Worked better than a bullet."

"It frightened everyone," Bess said softly. "It even made the stories about Frenchy's ghost somehow believable."

"It stopped work on the wire," Jim said. "Which was the main purpose behind the killings."

"You know who did it?" Mrs. Orville's voice was bitter.

"Not yet." Jim finished his coffee and stood up. "I don't mean to keep you, but I have to make sure of easement rights. We're going through Frenchy's Canyon. I understand your husband negotiated a right-of-way with the heirs in New Orleans?"

Mrs. Orville nodded. "There's a copy of the agreement in Paul Saint's office. We have the original here."

"Why the copy to Paul Saint?"

Mrs. Orville hesitated. "My husband didn't get along too well with Mr. Saint."

"Didn't trust him, you mean?"

She took a moment, then answered bluntly,

105

"No, he didn't." She got up. "You want the paper?"

"I think it's safer with you," he said.

"You look a bit like Bill, but I wouldn't take you for his brother," she said. She waited for a comment, but Jim didn't make any and she went on, "You're harder than he was. But maybe that's what it takes to live out here."

She and Bess walked with Jim to the door.

Bess was like her mother, direct and frank. "Why did you go to South America?"

Jim hesitated.

Mrs. Orville answered for him, "I guess some men just can't stay put in their own back yard, can they, Jim?"

"I guess that's it," Jim said. He looked at Bess. "I was down in Mexico and wound up in Vera Cruz. There was a ship in the harbor, and"—he smiled—"I had never been aboard a ship. It happened to be going to Buenos Aires."

Bess nodded. "I understand."

Mrs. Orville looked at her daughter. "I'm glad you do. I never could." Her gaze came back to Jim. "The work of this world is done by the men who stay put."

Jim grinned. "Where are you going, Mrs. Orville?"

"Call me Kathy," she said. "Your brother did." She made a motion toward the outside. "That sign's coming down tonight. We're going to stay right here, in Junction City—"

Bess stared at her. "Ma—?"

The older woman cut her off. "I just made up my mind." She looked at Jim. "Be a good idea if you settled down yourself, Jim."

"I might," Jim said. He was looking at Bess. "After we run this wire through to Fort Cochise for Mr. Simpson."

He opened the door and said, "Good night."

"Come again," Mrs. Orville said.

She watched Jim go down the path to the gate, then closed the door and looked at Bess. "He could make a good husband."

"Not with you pushing him into it," Bess said.

Kathy Orville smiled. "I'll stay out of it." She turned. "Come—we've got a lot of unpacking to do. . . ."

Mike Donovan stopped at the desk and asked the clerk if he had seen the man who had signed for a room as Walter Evans. The desk clerk shook his head. But the Trans-Pecos construction boss had paid for his room a week in advance and it was still ready for him.

"If he comes in tonight, tell him I want to see him," Donovan said, and laid a four-bit piece on the counter.

"Yes, sir," the clerk said brightly. He watched the big man cross the lobby to the door. Donovan's suit was expensive, but somehow the big Overland boss would always look better in a tough hickory shirt and work pants.

Donovan paused on the walk in front of the hotel, feeling the pull of his powerful shoulders against his coat. He still smarted at the way Paul Saint had managed to ease out of what should have been an awkward situation for him and his new construction boss.

He took a fresh cigar from his coat pocket and lighted it, turning his back to the cold wind. Jim Davis had to be in town. It was a long ride back to Cottonwood camp and there was no reason for him to have gone back tonight.

He turned his gaze to the building line beyond the hotel. Probably in one of the saloons. Donovan rubbed the knuckles of his right hand into the palm of his left and smiled in anticipation. Sooner or later he'd find him. . . .

The Railroad Bar was the third place he tried. He walked inside, paused to look over the few quiet customers at the tables. Hank, the deputy, was sitting alone, a bottle of whiskey almost empty in front of him. His gaze came up to meet Donovan's and he settled back in his chair, his smile a bit blurred.

Donovan walked directly to the bar, ordered a whiskey and asked a question. He asked it loud and clear.

"I'm looking for Trans-Pecos' new construction boss. Anyone see him?"

The bartender shook his head. He filled Donovan's glass and moved away. The Overland man was plainly looking for trouble, and the last thing the bartender wanted was a fracas in his place.

Donovan turned on his elbow and stared at the few men in the saloon. His eyes hit them with frank challenge. He was a big Irishman with crisp curly black hair beginning to gray. His stomach bulged a little over his belt, but his arms were still thick and hard and there was muscle under the layers of stomach fat.

One of the saloon girls, attracted by his town clothes and heavy gold watch chain which suggested money, came up to him. She smiled falsely. "Buy a little girl a big drink, mister?"

Donovan looked her over, making his male inventory with an experienced eye. "Some other time," he said. "I'm looking for different entertainment tonight."

The girl pouted. "It's cold outside." She snuggled closer. "It's warm upstairs."

He pushed her away and beckoned to the bartender. "Give this lady a great big bottle of whiskey." He tossed a gold piece on the counter. "And let her keep the change." The girl took the bottle and the money and went back to join her companions. In the morning she'd exchange the whiskey for the rest of the money.

Donovan picked up his glass and walked to

Hank's table. Hank leaned back, eyed him. He lifted his own half-filled glass as Donovan sat down.

"Mr. Michael Donovan," he said. His voice was a little blurred. "How's murder?"

Donovan frowned. Then he noticed that Hank wasn't wearing a badge, nor his gunbelt, and that he was quite drunk. He relaxed.

"How's the law?" he said, using the same light vein.

Hank blinked owlishly. "What law?" He looked around the room, squinting. "When you find it, Mr. Donovan, let me know."

Donovan's smile slipped from his lips. He didn't like this kind of foolish talk.

"You seen Davis around?"

Hank wagged his head. "Was in Paul Saint's house last I saw him. You were there."

"He's got a room at the hotel, but he hasn't checked in yet. I looked."

"What do you want him for?"

Donovan shrugged. "Just a few questions. I didn't want to embarrass Mr. Saint in his house. And the sheriff seemed satisfied. But—" he studied Hank—"he said he found Walter Evans dead. How come he didn't bring the body into town himself? And if he didn't kill him, who did?"

Hank chuckled. "I was going to ask you that, Mr. Donovan. But the sheriff said no." The

110

deputy finished his whiskey. "Don't care who kills who, he said . . . just stay out of it."

Donovan leaned back in his chair. "Sorry he feels that way," he said. He didn't really, but he wanted the statement on record.

"What are you doing in town?" Hank asked. "Overland isn't doing any business here."

Donovan looked at the deputy without expression. "Just visiting," he said.

He got up and walked back toward the bar. He was beginning to feel a letdown. He pushed his empty glass toward the bartender. "Once more," he said.

Jim entered as the bartender poured Donovan his drink. Mike saw him in the mirror—a tall man, lean at the hips, wide in the shoulders; there was a hard, rawhide toughness about Jim that came through only after a first look. And Donovan noticed now the way Davis came into the saloon, pausing for a moment just inside, a catlike alertness holding him—it was the way men like Spade and Grady came into a bar. . . .

The bartender spotted Jim at the same time and his hand trembled as he set the bottle down. He said in a quick low voice, "I hope there won't be any trouble, Mr. Donovan."

"That'll be up to Mr. Davis," Donovan said. He turned then, his back braced against the bar.

"Davis!" he said sharply. "I've been looking for you!"

111

Jim Davis walked to the bar. "So I heard," he said. His eyes measured the big man and he knew immediately what Donovan was after.

Donovan made a casual gesture to the worried bartender. "A drink for Mr. Davis."

He turned back to Jim as the bartender poured. "You know why I'm looking for you?"

Jim shrugged. "My brother used to talk about you. Said you were like those grizzlies from up north, always had to stand taller than the rest."

Donovan's eyes lighted. "I licked your brother twice."

"So he told me."

Davis reached out and took the cigar from Donovan's lips and dropped it into Donovan's glass. "Let's get it over with," he said bleakly.

Donovan looked at his whiskey glass, then at Jim. His eyes flared with a wicked light. "I don't carry a gun," he said distinctly.

Jim unbuckled his holster, handed it across the bar to the bartender. As he started to turn back, Donovan hit him.

The blow spun Jim back into the nearest table. Donovan went after him with a roar, swinging with both hands. Jim went down, twisting and avoiding most of Donovan's blows. He barely rolled out of the way in time as Donovan jumped for him, both feet coming down hard.

Jim kicked out, staggering Donovan. It gave him a chance to regain his feet as Donovan came charging back. Jim jammed the heel of his right hand hard against Donovan's chin, snapping the man's head back. He chopped down with the hard side of his palm against the base of Donovan's bull neck. Donovan stumbled, his left arm suddenly useless. As he turned Jim hit him twice, rocking his head around. As Donovan's knees momentarily buckled, Jim brought his knee up into the Overland man's face.

Blood gushed from Donovan's broken nose. He reeled back against a table, sagged. Jim gripped him by the shoulders and ran him back toward the bar. He rammed Donovan's head against the walnut timbers and the big man collapsed, sprawling limply across the brass railing.

Jim straightened and wiped blood from the cut on his lip. His left eye would be half-closed in the morning. He walked back to where his hat lay, picked it up. The bartender wordlessly handed him his gunbelt and he buckled it about his waist.

Behind Jim, Hank rose unsteadily to his feet. He walked to where Donovan lay crumpled, then turned to Jim. He seemed suddenly quite sober.

"Kill him?"

Jim shook his head.

Hank began to laugh . . . it had a bitter ring. "You should have. Then his men would kill you. Everything between Trans-Pecos and Overland. Solve all our problems."

Jim eyed him, frowning.

113

The bartender came around the counter. "Time to go home, Hank." He looked at Jim, hoping Davis wouldn't object.

Hank tried to shake him off. "Leave me alone, Lou. I want to stay and see the fun when Donovan's men come after him."

"They won't be in tonight," Lou said. He took Hank's arm. "Come on, Hank. You said you wanted to go home when you finished the bottle."

Hank pulled his arm free, turned to look back to his table. The bottle was empty. "Well, whaddya know?" He gave into the bartender. "All right, Lou—give me my gunbelt."

The bartender shook his head. "Pick it up tomorrow."

He led Hank toward the door.

Hank twisted, looked back to Jim. "I'll be up bright and early," he promised. "Don't want to miss the fun. . . ."

Lou gently pushed him through the doorway.

Davis shrugged. He went behind the bar, filled a pitcher with cold beer. He walked back to stand over Donovan, and slowly began to pour the beer down the back of the big man's neck.

XIII

The cold night wind steadied Hank somewhat. He braced his feet and took in a deep lungful of air and turned to the bartender. "All right, Lou—I can make it from here."

Lou hesitated. "You sure?"

Hank nodded. He pushed away from the bartender, clung briefly to a porch support to get his bearings, then turned and waved Lou inside.

"Damn it, Lou—I said I'm all right!"

The bartender stood in the doorway for a moment, then shrugged and went inside.

Hank stumbled across the street to the law office. No sense in waking everybody up at the boardinghouse, he thought. He'd sleep on the cot in one of the cells tonight. He started to fumble in his pockets for the law office keys. . . .

Three blocks away, Lee Watson rode cautiously through the cold night, keeping to the shadows. He was cold and tired and hungry. He had made no provisions for a long stay at Superstition Point and the longer he had waited for Paul Saint the more he had time to think.

He and Pete had been paid to kill Walter Evans, not to hide out. If anyone had reason to worry, it was Saint. One word from him to the sheriff and it would be Paul Saint on the run.

His silence should be worth more money to the Trans-Pecos division manager. Enough money, he thought greedily, to set him up for life in Mexico.

Most of the town was asleep as he came out to Railroad Avenue. Paul's house was to the east of the railroad station; he wondered if Saint would still be up.

Lee Watson felt edgy. The raw wind seemed to bite through his coat. He kept his gun hand thrust down into his coat pocket to keep it warm.

The law office was dark. Hank had probably gone home. He turned his attention to the saloon across the street, not noticing Hank in the deep shadows by the office. There were no horses tied up at the saloon rack. Probably no more than two or three people left in the place . . . a good time to stop in for a drink. And he needed a drink, Lee decided, before he faced Paul Saint.

He knew the slender, quiet Trans-Pecos man wouldn't like the shakedown. And there was something about the man that unsettled Lee . . . a quiet deadliness at odds with the boyish features and citified manners.

He turned his tired mount into the saloon rack, glanced up and down the deserted street. He dismounted, tied up. *One drink,* he told himself. *No one would notice. . . .*

Across the street, his back braced against the side of the building, Hank finally found his keys.

Beats hell how butterfingered a man gets when he's got a few drinks in him, the deputy thought.

He started for the door, but the keys slipped from his fingers as he tried to fit one into the lock. He cursed softly as he turned to pick them up.

He saw Lee Watson by the tie rack, but he did not recognize the man until Lee stepped into the splash of light from the saloon.

Hank suddenly forgot Sheriff Collins' warning; he only remembered that it had been Lee Watson who had brought the bodies of Evans and Pete Mallory into his office.

If Jim Davis had told a straight story, how had Watson known where to find the bodies?

He started across the street, stumbling down the steps, calling at the same time, "Lee!"

Almost at the saloon door, Lee whirled. He saw the deputy running toward him and he reacted instinctively. He drew and fired. . . .

Hank turned all the way around under the impact of the bullet. His right hand groped for the gun that was no longer at his hip. Then he fell.

Lee ran back to his horse. He could hear voices inside the saloon, the thud of boots heading for the door. He untied his animal, swung aboard. He was backing the horse away from the rack when Jim Davis broke out onto the veranda. Lee fired one hasty shot in his direction.

Jim's answering shot lifted Watson out of the saddle. He fell backward, sliding down off his animal's rump. Jim's bullet had gone through his shoulder, but it was his horse who killed him. He fell under the animal and tried to roll away as the horse panicked. A shod hoof came down on his face, a thousand pounds of horseflesh behind it.

No one tried to catch the animal as it ran down the street, away from the saloon.

Jim took one look at Lee Watson, then ran to Hank down in the middle of the street. Hank was still breathing.

The few men who had been in the saloon spilled out into the street. Lou, the bartender, pushed through, and stopped by Jim's side. He was holding Hank's gunbelt in his hands.

Jim said roughly, "He won't need that now. Give me a hand with him. We need to get him to a doctor."

Lou nodded. There were tears in his eyes. He handed Hank's gunbelt to a man at his elbow. "Someone wake up the sheriff. . . ."

He bent over the unconscious deputy and took hold of his legs. The stragglers followed him and Jim toward Doctor Sawyer's office.

The three scantily clad saloon girls stood in the doorway, shivering.

Donovan shoved them aside as he came out. He braced himself against the cut of the wind, looked out toward the group of men following Davis and Lou up the street. His glance fell on Lee Watson's body by the hitchrack.

"What happened?"

His voice was harsh, thick through puffed lips. There was blood on his face and on his clothes, and he reeked of beer. He had taken a savage beating and he knew what he looked like. He turned on them when they didn't answer and they shrank away from him.

One of the girls said, "There was a shooting . . ."

Donovan stared into the street. He didn't recognize Watson's body.

He took out a handkerchief and wiped some of the blood from his face. The girl who had approached him earlier came up to him now. "You can clean up in my room—"

He pushed her away and started down the steps. He had taken beatings before, and survived. But Jim Davis had made it look easy. And for this Donovan would never forgive him.

He stumbled up the dark street toward the hotel.

Sheriff Collins looked down at his deputy stretched out on the doctor's examining table. A film of sweat beaded Hank's forehead and upper lip. He was breathing heavily, like a man undergoing some hard physical exertion. But his eyes were closed and he was not aware of anyone in the room.

Collins' voice was strained. "How much chance does he have, Doc?"

Sawyer shook his head. "I can't promise anything. Bullet's in his left lung." He hesitated. "I can get it out. But he might die . . . of . . . other causes. . . ."

"He'll die if you don't!" Collins said harshly. "Take it out!"

Sawyer shrugged. He shrank from the responsibility, but he knew he would have to go through with it.

"I'll need Mrs. Murphy," he said. "She usually helps out on things like this."

Collins nodded. "You give Hank a fighting chance, Doc. That's all I ask."

He turned to Jim Davis and Lou, who were in the room with him; he made a gesture toward the door.

On the walk outside Lou turned to the sheriff. "I should have given Hank his gun," he said. He felt shaken over this; he had always liked the deputy.

"Wouldn't have done him any good if you had," Jim said quietly. "He was in no condition to use it."

Lou stood helpless. He felt responsible, somehow, for what had happened to Hank and nothing could be said to change it.

"Stop by Mrs. Murphy's place on your way back," the sheriff said, "and tell her Doc Sawyer needs her; make sure she understands it's urgent."

Lou nodded. He hung on for a moment, reluctant to leave, but knowing there was nothing he could do here. "I've got his badge, Vic—"

Collins interrupted him. "Give it back to Hank when he's better."

He watched Lou walk off, then turned to face Jim. "So you gave Mike Donovan a beating tonight?" It was as much a statement as a question and he didn't expect an answer. He sighed heavily.

"I didn't want to get involved in a wire company fight," he said. "I told Hank to stay out of it." He looked up at the dark, scurrying clouds. "Guess a man gets pushed into things he doesn't want, anyway."

"Sometimes," Jim said. He understood what Hank had said a little better now. "It's probably no secret that Donovan's in town to stop Trans-Pecos. He started with me tonight, but this isn't the end of it. There'll be more trouble." Jim looked directly at the sheriff. "I want to know where you stand."

"Right where the law always stands," Collins replied bitterly. "In the middle."

"What does that mean?"

"If I move against Donovan, Overland will put pressure on me. Next thing I know I'll be out of a job." He made a gesture of resignation. "It's not the job so much, although I'm getting too old to

121

do much else. But losing the badge wouldn't help you."

He looked off down the dark street. "It's between you and Mike Donovan," he said slowly. "There's nothing much I can do about it. . . ."

"I'll keep that in mind, sheriff." Jim started to move away.

The sheriff stepped down beside him. "I had a look at the man you shot. His face is a mess, but I think he's Lee Watson. He's the man who brought Evans' body in . . . and Pete Mallory's." He frowned slightly. "He and Pete hung around town together. He disappeared right after he brought the bodies in. Hank wanted to ask him a few questions—"

"I should have," Jim broke in. "He and Mallory were on the train with Evans . . . one or the other shot him."

The two men stopped in front of the hotel. The sheriff said, "I'll try to stop any killing in town, but—"

"Thanks." Jim's voice was dry.

Collins chose to ignore the faint edge of contempt in Davis' voice.

"Mike Donovan probably hired Pete and Lee to kill Evans," Collins said. "But there's no way now that we can prove it."

"I don't think Donovan did," Jim said.

Vic looked sharply at him, frowning. "Who else would?"

"I'll tell you when I know for sure." Jim looked up as a half moon began to show through rifts in the heavy clouds.

"Clearing up." Jim's smile had an iron hardness. "Give us two weeks of good weather and we'll be in Fort Cochise on schedule."

Collins studied him for a moment, then shrugged. "If Donovan lets you," he said.

He moved on then, his stride heavy and without hope.

XIV

Dick Rainer tucked his rifle under his right arm and brought his cold hands up to his mouth, cupping them and trying to blow warmth into numbed fingers. His entire body felt stiff and uncomfortable. It was early morning and he had not yet warmed up to the day which promised to be better.

The sun poked through the low clouds, sending a shaft of light through the blackened ruins of Frenchy's ranchhouse. Dick let his glance run over the charred timbers. They could have slept in the barn last night, away from the raw bite of the wind, but somehow no one had suggested it. There was that indefinable aura about this fire-gutted ranch that made men uneasy.

He didn't believe in ghosts. But no one had yet come up with an explanation of how Bill Davis, Steve Orville and Kemp Overton had died. And despite the new construction boss' assurances, he had slept little last night, listening to the wind whistle through Frenchy's lonely ruins. And he knew he had not been alone in his sleeplessness.

He'd be damn glad, he thought, when they moved away from here.

Twenty feet away the posthole diggers were already sweating, jamming heavy crowbars into the hard ground. Dick let his gaze run idly down their back stretch. Three feet down and fourteen feet up . . . a track of postholes and poles across a wilderness, carrying a single strand of wire to tie together isolated towns and provide almost instantaneous communications between them.

A dozen wire companies fighting for contracts, for rights-of-way, spreading tentacles of communication across a continent. A dozen companies that one day, through merger, amalgamation and financial failure, would end up as one giant concern controlling wire communications from coast to coast.

Dick swung his gaze past the sweating men to the cliff rising behind the gutted ranch house. Two more postholes and they'd be at the base of the cliff. Already a work crew had left Cottonwood camp, making the long run which would take them to the top of that barrier. From there they would erect a winch hoist to haul up poles and wire for the last long march to Fort Cochise.

Tom Shawn, thick-shouldered, graying straw boss of the three-man posthole crew, walked up to Rainer, mopping his brow with his big blue work handkerchief. He glanced back, downvalley.

"Wire stringers and pole setters should be catching up with us by noon. We'll wait for them here."

Rainer nodded. He turned his attention to the

cliff. "When do you expect Joe and the wagon crew to show up on top?"

Tom shrugged. "Tonight, maybe. If they don't kill their team, pushing them." He smiled reflectively. "Beats hell how some men can get you to kill yourself working for them."

Rainer frowned. "Who is he, anyway? Jack says he isn't Walter Evans—"

Tom shrugged. "I don't care who he is. He's getting this job done."

"Think Donovan will give us trouble?"

Tom eyed the boy. "Maybe. That's why you're here." He smiled then at the look in Dick's eyes. "Don't let it worry you. Nobody'll come here today."

Dick brought his cold hands up to his mouth again. The rifle slid down under his arm, jarring on the hard ground. He picked it up, looking shamefacedly at Tom.

"Still pretty stiff," he said. "I didn't sleep much last night. . . ."

Tom glanced at the fire-blackened ruins. "I don't think any of us did." He put a hand on Dick's shoulder. "Put that rifle down, run around a little. Better yet, give the boys a hand with that crowbar. That'll warm you up."

Dick grinned. He set the rifle down, propping its muzzle up against a nearby rock and went to join the diggers.

Tom walked on, past the ranch house, stopping

close to the base of the cliff. He had worked for Warren Simpson a long time, had dug holes for Trans-Pecos in all sorts of ground. He could see where, up the face of that almost sheer cliff, crevices could be widened, chipped deeper, a two-by-four jammed in, protruding just far enough to keep the wire from the abrasive action of the rock wall.

He nodded to himself. It could be done. He turned and started back and then stopped as he saw the two riders. They had appeared abruptly on the trail behind, and they were not anyone he recognized.

A faint alarm struck its note of warning in the blocky straw boss. He walked a little faster, reaching his crew before the oncoming riders.

They were intent on their work and had not noticed. Tom said quickly, "We've got company coming. . . ."

The men paused. Dick was handling the crowbar, the other two held shovels. Slowly Dick handed the crowbar to one of the men and turned—a small beading of sweat put a shine on his young face.

It was twenty feet to where he had left the rifle. He started to move toward it.

Spade cut his horse in between Dick and the rifle. He pulled up and looked down at the youngster, his voice cold. "Leave it alone, boy!"

Dick stopped.

Grady rode slowly past them to the men clustered around the porthole. He leaned forward in his saddle, surveyed the hole for a long moment, his face expressionless.

"Nice hole," he said finally. He smiled with his lips, but his eyes were icy and without humor. "Now let's fill it up."

No one moved.

Grady sighed. He drew his Colt and pointed the muzzle at Tom Shawn. "All right . . . you tell them, fella. Fill the hole!"

"No!" Shawn's voice was harsh. He started to take a step toward Grady. "Donovan can't—"

Grady's shot nicked Tom's heavy work shoe. Tom flinched, stepped back.

Grady said patiently, "After you get through with this one, we're going to backtrack, filling all the holes we passed on the way up here." He chuckled mirthlessly. "Aw, come on now, it won't be so bad. Just means more work for you—and more wages."

He studied them for a moment. "Look at it this way," he said. "It's the company's money, not yours."

One of the diggers said, "Hell with you, mister. You want this hole filled, you do it!"

Grady looked at him, eyes deadly. Slowly he cocked the hammer of his gun, turned the muzzle on the man. But he looked at Tom as he said, "All right, mister—it's up to you. You tell them. Or I fill that hole with his body!"

Tom nodded. "Do as he says." His voice was bitter.

Reluctantly the two men began shoveling rocks and dirt back into the hole. Grady eased the hammer back and started to slide his gun back into the holster.

Rainer looked at them. He had been placed here for just such an occasion, and he had failed. A day's work would be shot to hell . . . and they couldn't afford another delay.

Grady turned and made a motion to Spade and Spade started to edge his horse toward his companion. Grady said, "Maybe we ought to see what they have in the barn—?"

Spade nodded and swung around . . . for a moment his back was to Rainer and the boy made a break for the rifle.

Grady turned slightly in the saddle. He deliberately let Rainer get his hands on the weapon and turn around . . . then he drew and fired.

Dick went over backward, the rifle flying out of his hands.

One of the diggers cursed, and lunged at Grady, swinging his shovel. Grady shot him.

Tom and the other digger didn't move. Spade rode slowly to where Dick lay on his back. He glanced down at the boy, then swung away and rejoined Grady.

He looked at Tom. "Let's get to work!"

The afternoon sun filtered through the gutted timbers of Frenchy's ranch house and across the hard faces of the men grouped about Dick Rainer's blanket-covered body. They were watching Jim Davis—waiting for his orders.

Jack Sanders made a bitter gesture. "The kid's dead. Regis has a bullet in him, but maybe he'll live." He looked off down the valley, a helpless anger in his eyes. "Just plain murder, that's what it was."

Jim crouched beside Dick's body and lifted a corner of the blanket from the kid's face. Behind him Tom Shawn said stonily, "Dick didn't have a chance. He shouldn't have tried it."

Jim let the blanket fall back over Dick and straightened slowly. His eye was half closed and the bruise under it was livid.

"I figured Donovan would hit us," he said. "But not so soon . . ."

He turned and studied this Trans-Pecos crew. Some of them had been in company fights before.

"I'm sorry about the kid," he said. "And about Regis. But Donovan made his point. We can quit now. Trans-Pecos folds and Overland takes over." He smiled grimly. "Some of you might even be offered jobs by Donovan—"

"To hell with Overland!" a man said. He looked at the others, daring them to say different.

Jack Sanders said, "Nobody's quitting, Evans. But we can't stand up to Donovan without protection—"

"There's rifles and shotguns for every man in the wagon I drove in from town," Jim cut in. "From now on every man works with a gun by his side."

He turned to Tom Shawn. "The man who killed the kid—you can identify him?"

Tom's eyes brightened. "Damn well I can!"

"You ride?"

Tom nodded. "I can hang on long enough to get to town."

Jim pointed. "Get a saddle on one of those horses. Wait for me."

Shawn moved away from the group.

Jim swung around to Sanders. "We got one break, anyway. The weather's clearing. There'll be a moon out tonight. Enough light to work by." His voice was hard. "I want to see Trans-Pecos wire strung up to the base of that cliff when I return tomorrow."

Jack nodded. Then, as Jim started to turn away he said sharply, "Wait!" He walked slowly to Davis, looked hard at him. "You're not Walter Evans. Who are you?"

"Bill Davis' brother, Jim."

Sanders stared at him.

"Evans is dead," Jim said. "I took his place. It turned out not to be a very good idea."

"Paul Saint know?"

"He does now," Jim said. "So does Donovan." He touched the bruise under his eye and smiled grimly. "I said handling trouble was my business, Jack. You get that wire strung."

Sanders eyed the gun at Jim's hip.

"Donovan came looking for a fight last night," Jim said bleakly, "and he got one. Now he's pushing for a war. All right, we'll give it to him!"

XV

Sheriff Collins stood uncomfortably at the foot of the small bed and looked at his deputy. Hank was conscious, his chest swathed in bandages. A fever thermometer protruded from between his clenched lips.

Collins managed a cheerful smile. "You'll be up in no time," he said. "Just take it easy. You're still on the payroll."

Hank's clouded eyes sought the sheriff's face. He tried to lift a hand in answer to Vic, but it was too much of an effort.

Mrs. Murphy, a buxom, cheerful widow disposed to helping others, took the thermometer from Hank's mouth, glanced at it, then handed it to Dr. Sawyer. The doctor read it, frowned slightly, shook it and put it back in a small glass containing alcohol.

"Take his temperature every hour," he told her. He turned to the sheriff, made a slight head motion toward the door.

Collins said, "I'll drop in again this afternoon, Hank."

In the hallway outside, Dr. Sawyer said bluntly, "I cut the bullet out without too much damage to his lung. But like I said, he's beginning to run a fever . . ." He took a breath. "Now the rest is up to him."

Collins nodded. "He'll come through it." Somehow he had this confidence in Hank.

But he had little confidence in himself as he left the doctor's house and walked toward his office. Hank had been right, of course. It was demeaning to find out that in times of real trouble they could do little except stand on the sidelines and watch.

It *was* a matter for federal law enforcement, he told himself. Let them send a U.S. marshal here. . . .

But he knew he had sent for government help a little too late. He should have written that letter as soon as Mike Donovan showed up: he had known then how it would be.

Down the street the morning train whistled its approach. He paused in front of his office door to watch as it pulled up by the small station.

His glance ran disinterestedly over the first debarking passengers. But the men who emerged from the last car, the smoker, held his attention sharply.

They were a burly, strong-arm group in ill-fitting and cheap town clothes led by a tall man who left no doubt as to his calling. The gunbelts crossed at his flat stomach and the holsters were thonged down low on his thighs.

They picked up small battered handbags which

they had carried with them aboard the train, and which appeared to be all the baggage they had, and started directly for the hotel.

They crossed the street in a group, passing by the law officer on their way. Each man looked at Collins as they went by, eyeing the badge on his coat and dismissing him. Collins felt the heat of their disrespect against the back of his neck.

For a fleeting instant he wanted to stop them, ask them their business . . . he wanted to make them aware that there was law in Junction City. But the feeling dissipated immediately, leaving him with a shame he would never overcome.

He saw Paul Saint watch the group from the window of the Trans-Pecos office and he sought refuge in what he had told Hank.

This trouble was between Trans-Pecos and Overland—and it would be up to the federal law enforcement office to sort out the guilt afterward. It would go into the courts, with Warren Simpson and the men behind Overland facing each other behind batteries of attorneys. But by then Trans-Pecos would be ruined and men would be killed. . . .

His step was heavy as he turned and went into his office.

The hotel clerk looked across the small lobby to the group of men coming toward him. He was used to all sorts of men seeking accommodations here, but the tall man with the two guns held his attention. About forty, he judged, graying at the temples . . . a quiet man with a contemplative look in his gray eyes, the marks of refinement subtly clinging.

They stopped in front of the desk. The tall man spoke for all of them.

"Mr. Donovan's expecting us. I'm Len Petersen."

"Yes, sir," the clerk said. "Mr. Donovan has reserved rooms." He turned and plucked keys from a board at his back. "Sorry some of you will have to double up. We are short . . ."

Petersen handed keys to the thick blond man next to him. "Get the men settled, Wotjek. Then meet me at the bar." He looked at the clerk. "You have a bar in the hotel?"

"Yes, sir," the clerk snapped back. "Right on through that archway." He pointed.

The men picked up their bags and followed Wotjek up the stairs.

Len eyed the box of cigars on the counter, selected one. "Where is Mr. Donovan?"

"In room 308. He said for you to go right up."

Petersen went up the stairs and down a short hallway and knocked on Donovan's door. Donovan's voice punched through the panels. "Sure, come in."

The gunman entered a semi-dark room and paused. There were two windows in the big room, but the shades of both had been pulled down.

Donovan was sitting on the horsehair sofa—he had been lying down. He made a motion to Petersen.

"Come in, dammit. And shut the door."

Petersen kicked the door shut behind him, walked to the nearest window, and started to raise the blind.

Donovan cut him off. "Leave it alone!"

Petersen turned. "I like to see who I talk to," he said coldly. He raised the blind halfway, then walked to Donovan. "I'm Len Petersen," he said.

Donovan's swollen eyes were squinting. He said, "Dammit, I want those blinds down. Sun hurts my eyes."

Petersen smiled faintly. He could see now that Donovan's face was badly battered.

He walked back to the window and pulled the shade down. Donovan muttered, "Thanks," and waved to a bottle of whiskey he kept on the small table.

"Pour yourself a drink, Len."

Petersen ignored the invitation. He looked at Donovan. "I can come back later."

Donovan made a gesture. "Don't let this fool you. I've been through worse." He got up and poured himself a glass of whiskey, then one for Petersen.

"Ten years ago I could have taken him. Maybe even five . . ."

He handed the glass to Petersen who studied

Donovan's stocky figure. "Guess you could have. Who is he?"

"Name's Jim Davis."

Petersen was lifting the glass to his lips. He paused, a small shock in his eyes.

"Jim Davis? Tall as me . . . ten years younger? Dark hair, blue eyes, small tattoo on his left forearm?"

Donovan frowned. "Don't know about the tattoo. Rest of it fits."

Petersen's eyes held a sudden small and cynical light. "Well, wouldn't you know?"

"What did you say?"

"Nothing." Petersen walked to the window, pulled the shade back a bit and looked out. "I know him," he said. "He told me once he had a brother working for Trans-Pecos. But the last time I saw him he was in Vera Cruz."

"Well, he's here now!" Donovan growled. "Tougher than I expected." He eyed Petersen. "Think you can handle him?"

Petersen considered for a moment. "I can," he said. "But I don't know if I want to."

"Don't want to!" Donovan's voice was puzzled. "You were hired—"

"I wasn't told it would be Jim Davis."

Donovan stared at him. "What does it matter who it is?" Then, angrily: "You afraid of him?"

Petersen looked at him through gray, icy eyes. Donovan stiffened. "Then why?"

138

"I didn't say I wouldn't take the job," Petersen said. "I'll have to think it over."

Donovan shrugged. "Go ahead. But don't take too much time." He walked to the table and put his glass down. His head was beginning to ache and he felt like lying down.

"I sent two men out last night to do a job. They should be back in town this afternoon." He looked at Petersen. "If they did their job right, Jim Davis should be coming after them before night."

He eyed the tall, silent gunman. "Spade and Grady," he said. "You know them?"

Petersen shook his head.

Donovan frowned. "Spade's good with a gun. So is Grady." He took a deep breath. "Maybe we won't need you, anyway."

"You'll need me." Petersen walked to the door. "If Jim Davis comes looking for them, your men better leave town."

He went out, closing the door behind him.

Donovan touched the bruises under his eyes. He didn't know Len Petersen, but already he disliked the man. Jim Davis couldn't be that good with a gun. And he had a lot of faith in Spade and Grady.

The others were waiting for Petersen when he walked into the hotel bar.

Wotjek, with a heavy Polish face and broken nose, asked, "When do we go to work?"

139

"Later . . . maybe."

Wotjek frowned. "Later?" He glanced toward the lobby. "Where is Mr. Donovan?"

"In his room." Petersen smiled faintly. "He isn't seeing anyone right now."

Wotjek was concerned. "Sick?"

"Yeah." Petersen tossed some money on the bar. "Drinks on me, until this runs out."

Wotjek looked after him as Petersen turned away. "What do we do, Mr. Petersen?"

"Wait."

Petersen went out, stopped on the walk in front of the hotel. The sun was bright in the sky, with no clouds to mar it; the morning was pleasantly warm. He took out the cigar he had taken from the hotel counter and lighted up, then he started for the Trans-Pecos office across the street.

Ellen Saint was at a desk, going over supply invoices, when Petersen walked in. She looked up and a shock went through her, causing her to drop her pencil.

For a moment it looked as though Jim Davis had walked in, yet she could plainly see that this man was older and didn't really look like Jim at all. But something, the way he wore his guns, the quiet, confident way he had about him . . .

She got up and walked to the low railing separating them. "Yes?" she said. "Do you wish to send a wire?"

Petersen looked her over before he answered.

140

He did it quietly and she could find no offense in the gleam of admiration that flitted through his eyes.

"No, ma'am," he replied. "I'm just looking for a man."

Ellen smiled. "Well, I don't believe I can help—"

She broke off as Paul Saint came in from the warehouse. Paul stopped as he saw Petersen, a quick alertness tightening his face. Then he came forward, a clipboard and tally sheet in his hand, and joined them.

"I'm Paul Saint, division manager," he said curtly to Petersen. "What can I do for you?"

Petersen studied Paul for a moment, revising his first appraisal as he looked deeper into Paul's cold eyes. "I'm looking for a man I was told works for Trans-Pecos," he said. "His name is Jim Davis."

Ellen started slightly.

A gleam came into Paul's eyes. "Yes," he said coldly. "Davis works for Trans-Pecos. What do you want him for?"

Petersen shrugged. "I'll tell him when I see him."

Fear prompted Ellen's quick comment. "He isn't here. We don't know where he is."

Petersen looked at her, then at Paul. "I'll find him. But you could save me a lot of time."

"Who are you?" Paul's voice was brusque.

141

"An old friend of Jim's. Name's Petersen." He said it casually and was glad when he saw that it made no sharp impression on Paul Saint or the woman.

Paul took a considering breath. "Well, if you're a friend . . ." He made a gesture toward the outside. "You should find Davis at our Cottonwood Creek camp."

He gave Petersen directions how to get there.

Petersen said, "Thank you." He tipped his hat politely to Ellen, and went out.

Ellen turned to Paul, the small fear lingering in her. "He could be one of Donovan's men—"

"He probably is," Paul said. He turned and left her and she watched him go to his desk, pick up some papers and head back for the warehouse.

Petersen stopped in at the town stables, rented a saddle horse, and rode out of town, following the creek road.

He passed Spade and Grady about five miles out. They were riding toward a narrow plank bridge across the Cottonwood. Spade and Grady would have made the bridge first, but Spade suddenly crowded his horse against Grady's forcing him to one side.

Grady snarled, "What the hell—?"

But Spade's fingers, tightening on his arm, stopped him. They waited as Petersen crossed and Spade nodded as the gunman came abreast of them.

Petersen gave Spade a look, but it was obvious he didn't recognize him. He rode on and Spade waited until the gunman had gone out of sight around a bend. Then he turned to Grady. "That's Len Petersen," he said. "I saw him once, down in El Paso."

Grady turned to look after Petersen. "Where's he headed?"

Spade shrugged. "That's his business."

They rode on toward town, and Donovan.

Petersen rode at a ground-eating jog and he made the Cottonwood camp just past noon. Moss, the telegrapher, came out of his tent as he approached. Two other men, loading a wagon, picked up rifles.

Petersen dismounted, ignoring the leveled guns, and walked toward Moss.

"I'm looking for a man name of Jim Davis," he said.

Moss frowned. "You come to the wrong place, mister. There's no one by that name here."

Petersen's glance took in the all but deserted camp. "I was told there was," he said. "Man name of Paul Saint, in town, told me."

Moss shook his head. "Must be some mistake. Nobody name of Davis here."

One of the men with rifles started to work the lever of the Winchester.

Petersen whirled. No one saw the gun that came into his hand. But it was there, as if by magic, the bullet tugging at the crown of the man's hat, boring its twin holes in it.

"The second one goes through your belt buckles," he said softly, "if you don't drop that rifle."

The man dropped his Winchester as though it had turned red-hot. So did the other rifleman.

Petersen eyed them for a moment, then slid his Colt back into its holster.

"All right," he said to Moss. "I guess Jim isn't here." He started to walk back to his horse, but stopped as the wagons came into sight.

Jack Sanders was on the seat of the first wagon. They pulled up by the tents and Sanders jumped down and walked toward Moss.

"We got a man hurt, in the wagon," he said grimly. "Wire Paul Saint. Tell him to send Doc Sawyer out right away. And—"

He paused as he saw Moss looking at Petersen. He turned and eyed the gunman, scowling.

Moss said, "This man's looking for someone named Jim Davis. I told him we didn't have anybody—"

Sanders cut him off. "What do you want with Davis?" he asked Petersen.

Petersen shrugged. His glance went to the half dozen men who had come back with Sanders . . . all of them were armed.

"I've got something that belongs to him. I came to give it to him."

Sanders eyed the tall gunman. "You know Davis?"

Petersen nodded. "We rode together in Mexico."

Sanders made a gesture down the road. "Jim's on his way to town. If you make a run for it you might catch up with him."

Petersen frowned. "I came in from Junction City. How'd I miss him?"

"He took the old road in from Frenchy's Canyon."

Petersen nodded. He mounted and now Jack Sanders said worriedly, "You're a friend of his, aren't you?"

Petersen gave him a small, indefinite smile. "We were," he said. He swung his mount away and rode off.

Moss came up by Sanders. "Who's Davis?"

Sanders was still looking after the gunman. He turned now and said wearily, "I'll tell you later. Right now we got a lot of work to do."

XVI

Mike Donovan was eating a late dinner in his room when Spade and Grady came in. He was feeling better, but the inside of his mouth was cut up and swollen and he had trouble eating.

"You're back early," he said. "How'd it go?"

Donovan had eased the window shades up halfway and there was enough light for Spade and Grady to notice his battered face, but neither man commented on it.

"We had to kill one of them," Spade said.

Donovan dropped his fork across his plate. "I thought we agreed—"

"He went for his rifle," Grady cut in. "I had to kill him."

Donovan frowned. "Since when has Trans-Pecos been arming its crew?"

Grady shrugged.

Spade said, "I saw Petersen. He was on his way to the Trans-Pecos camp on the Cottonwood. What's he going there for?"

Donovan shook his head. "You'll have to ask him." He wiped his lips gingerly with his napkin and pushed his plate away. He had lost his appetite.

"I don't know what he's doing—I don't even know if he's working for us. I told the front office to send Wotjek and the boys—I didn't send for Petersen."

He got up and walked to the window to look out. For a long moment no one said anything. Then Donovan turned.

"All right—you did what you had to. There's a train leaving in twenty minutes. Get on it."

Spade and Grady exchanged glances. Spade said slowly, "Why?"

"Because if Jim Davis shows up here, he'll kill you!"

Spade smiled. "He'll try, Mike."

"He'll kill you!" Mike's voice was flat. He came up to the two men, made a small gesture of friendliness. "Look—we've been together for a long time now. I don't want to see you get killed."

Spade's eyes narrowed angrily. "Mike—" he began.

Donovan put a hand on his shoulder. "The big boys at Overland sent Petersen. Let him handle Davis. That's why he's here."

Spade shook his head. "We're not running from anybody, Mike. You know us better than that."

"I talked to Petersen," Mike said. "Neither of you are fast enough to face Davis."

Grady grinned. "We won't have to be, Mike. Only one of us will face him."

Donovan frowned. "Who?"

"Me," Grady said. "I killed the kid, shot up the

other man. Davis will be looking for both of us, but he'll want me first. I'll make it easy for him to find me."

Mike looked at both of them. "You sure you know what you're doing?"

Grady nodded. "We've got a few tricks of our own, Mike. You just keep the sheriff in line."

"Collins won't bother you," Donovan promised.

"We'll handle Davis," Grady said. He pointed toward the window. "You can watch the show from here."

The sun moved down in the western sky and its warmth began to fade. A cooler wind blew in from the east.

Davis and Tom Shawn pulled up at the edge of town to give their animals a breather. Tom needed the rest more than the horse, but he tried not to show it. He had been bounced and jostled on a hard saddle for more miles than he wanted to remember and his entire backside was numb.

"No," he said slowly, in reply to Jim's question, "we didn't find anything. Your brother and Steve were lying on the road, about a hundred yards apart. Wasn't a mark on them, far as we could see." He frowned. "Of course, none of us did much looking . . . we were pretty well scared—" He paused, eyeing Jim, puzzled. "What should we have looked for?"

"A small dart," Jim said. "Maybe not bigger than a wood match."

Shawn shook his head. "We didn't see anything. But, like I said, we weren't looking."

"They could have been picked up before you got there," Jim said. He was looking off toward town, his eyes cold and remote.

Shawn scratched his head. "A dart? One that size couldn't kill—"

"The ones I'm thinking of could," Jim said.

Tom looked closely at him, but Davis offered nothing more, and after a moment Tom said, "They were Donovan's men. But Mike will deny it."

Davis' eyes had a wintry look. "Sure," he said softly. "But let's ask him, anyway."

Paul Saint, standing by the office windows, saw them ride in. He stepped out and called, "Davis!"

Jim and Shawn turned their mounts into the Trans-Pecos office. They did not dismount.

Paul said, "I just got word from Cottonwood camp." His voice was harsh. "Dick Rainer is dead. One of the men, Regis, is shot and needs a doctor."

Jim nodded. "I told Sanders to notify you."

Paul made an angry gesture. "I told you what to expect. You can't stop Donovan with guns."

Shawn's voice was hard. "Begging your pardon, Mr. Saint, but there ain't any other way, is there?"

Saint turned his gaze on the blocky man. "You can quit," he said coldly. "It's up to you and the others to decide if getting this wire through to Fort Cochise is worth your lives, Tom."

Tom said angrily, "We'll not be bullied into quitting, Mr. Saint."

"But you would?" Jim said to Paul. "Wouldn't you?"

"How many men do you want killed, Davis?" Paul's voice had a sneer in it. "What does Trans-Pecos mean to you, anyway?"

"Personally, nothing." Jim leaned forward, his eyes studying Paul. "But I took the job—and I'll see it finished."

He started to swing his horse away. Paul called after him, smiling coldly, "There was a man in town, Davis—looking for you."

Davis looked back at him. "Who?"

Paul shrugged. "Just said he was an old friend. I sent him to Cottonwood camp. You must have missed him."

Jim nodded. "If he's a friend, he'll find me."

He swung away from the office, with Shawn beside him. They rode across the street to the hotel and dismounted.

Shawn wobbled and clung to the saddle for a moment, looking at Jim. "Give me a minute," he groaned. "Gotta get some feeling back in my legs."

Jim looked up the street, to the law office. He

150

could go to the sheriff with Shawn, but Collins had told him where he stood last night and he had no reason to believe he had changed his mind today.

Shawn clumped stiffly to his side. "I'm a pick and shovel man," he said, "and from now on I'll do my riding in a wagon."

Donovan was standing by his window when they knocked on his door. He said, "Come on in," and turned to face them.

Davis looked around the big room. Donovan said mildly, "Looking for someone?"

"Two men," Jim said. "They work for you."

"Spade and Grady?" Donovan frowned. "What do you want with them?"

Shawn said harshly, "You know damned well what we want! They rode in on us at Frenchy's Canyon this morning. One of them killed a boy named Dick Rainer."

Donovan shook his head. "Not my men. Spade and Grady spent the night in Rincon. They just got back."

Jim's smile was bleak. "You've got witnesses to back them?"

Donovan's smile hurt him. "Of course."

Shawn balled his fist and took a step toward the Overland man. "You're a damn liar—"

Jim pulled him back.

Donovan said, "Don't start anything you can't finish, Davis."

151

Jim looked pointedly at him. "I never do."

He and Shawn went out. Donovan waited a moment, then crossed to the window. He had a good view of the street below.

"You won't finish it," he muttered, "not this time, Davis."

Grady sipped his beer slowly, making it last. He was a cold man, not given to emotion, but he felt the tug of impatience now. He had been in the Railroad Bar for almost an hour and he wanted to get it over with.

Lou came up and eyed Grady's glass and then walked away. A man who drank a glass and a half of beer in one hour was certainly not a drinking man.

Grady kept an eye on the door through the back bar mirror. It was getting late and he hadn't planned on facing Davis in the dark. *Maybe Davis isn't coming in,* he thought. But he knew Davis would be in and he was just fooling himself.

"I'll give him ten more minutes," he decided, realizing he had muttered the words out loud until the bartender turned to him and said, "Did you want another beer?"

Grady shrugged. "This one will do it." He lifted the glass to his lips and drained it; as he started to put the glass down he saw Jim and Tom Shawn come inside.

His hand shook a little as he set the glass

down and he made his voice casual. "On second thought, bartender, you better draw me another."

Davis glanced toward the bar as Tom pointed. He nodded, walked to Grady and tapped him on the shoulder. As Grady started to turn, Jim backhanded him across the mouth.

Grady staggered along the bar, nearly falling. He knuckled his split lip, eyes glinting. "What in the devil's gotten into you, mister?"

Jim turned to Tom. He asked the question distinctly, so everyone in the bar could hear it. "This the man who killed Dick Rainer, Tom?"

Tom nodded. "He's the man."

Grady looked at Shawn. "I don't know what you're talking about. I was in Rincon last night. I didn't kill anybody."

"So Donovan said," Jim answered. "He's a liar, and so are you."

Grady straightened, his back to the bar. "Mister," he said distinctly, "nobody calls me a liar!"

"I just did!" Jim said calmly.

Behind him men moved quickly out of gun range. But Grady grimly announced, "I'm not wearing a gun." Very carefully he eased back the skirt of his long coat to show Davis this was true.

"I'll give you five minutes to get one!" Jim's voice was fiat.

Grady nodded. "I'll be out in front of the hotel." He walked past Davis and Tom, and went out the door.

• • •

Spade was sitting on the bed when Grady entered their room. He had a rifle across his knees and he swiveled the muzzle toward the door as Grady came in.

Grady squirmed away and looked angrily at Spade, who muttered, "It's been a long wait. . . ."

"Hell of a time to get jumpy," Grady snarled. "I'm counting on you."

Spade reached over and picked up Grady's gunbelt, which had been resting on the bed beside him. He tossed it to his companion.

"Give me a few minutes to get set," he told Grady.

Grady nodded. "He's given me five." He smiled thinly at this as he buckled on his belt. "He won't know what hit him."

"Just don't rush things," Spade said. He levered a shell into place and went out, carrying the rifle.

Grady's hand shook slightly as he checked the rounds in his pistol. He cursed softly. He had never been this nervous before.

Len Petersen arrived in town a few minutes behind Davis. He turned his rented horse in at the stables and came back up the street toward the hotel.

It was late afternoon and the sun was low on the western hills, shining through a white cloud mist. The wind was turning cold.

The street appeared deserted and he thought, *I'm late,* and curiosity stirred in him. He wondered how Davis had made out, but it was a small emotion in him; it had been a long time since he had cared deeply about anything.

Then he saw Grady step out of the hotel, pause at the head of the steps and look toward the Railroad Bar. Petersen eased into a doorway. Grady was one of the two men he had met on the road to Cottonwood camp, and he had no doubt they were Donovan's men.

He waited for Spade to join Grady, but Grady was alone. He started down the stairs and Petersen glanced toward the bar and saw Davis and Tom Shawn come outside.

Shawn remained on the walk, a small group of men pushing out of the bar and around him. Davis stepped into the street and started walking toward the hotel.

Petersen watched Davis for a moment, his thoughts going back to another time and other places. It was the same kid he had taught to use a gun. Davis had learned well. But some things Petersen had taught him he seemed to have forgotten.

Petersen's gaze ranged along the street, behind Davis. He was looking for it and wasn't surprised when he caught the faint glint of a rifle and the blur of a man in an alley.

A man in front and one behind—and the kid was walking into it . . .

His fingers touched something hard and round in his pocket, and his eyes held a small sadness. *I should stay out of it,* he thought. But he knew he couldn't.

Jim Davis felt the tug of the cold wind against his coat. It made a lonely sound along the street, isolating him and bringing back, somehow, the sharp and bitter memories of a dry and windy day in Durango.

Like a hundred other Americans before him, he had hired out his gun in the cause of Mexican revolution and justice—only to find that in the quick-shifting politics of Mexico the peasant leader of today could be shot as the *bandido* tomorrow.

He had thrown in his lot with General Morales and they had been captured at Durango. It was luck that had given him a chance to escape; he never knew what had happened to the others.

A door opened somewhere up the street and he shook himself free of the past. It was a dangerous thing to do, he reflected, slipping back to another time, when ahead of him a man with a gun waited.

He saw that it was Sheriff Collins who had come out of his office. The lawman stood on the walk for a moment, a bitterness in his eyes.

Then he went back inside and closed the door.

Davis kept his gaze on Grady. The man was standing in the middle of the street, impersonal, waiting. His right hand swept back the tail of his coat, revealing the gun belted at his hip.

Jim stopped twenty-five feet away. Somewhere in town was this man's companion. Tom had warned him, but there was no time to find out now. He had pushed Grady into this, and Davis knew he had to take his chances.

"You've got your gun," he said impatiently. "Use it!"

"What's your hurry, mister?" Grady's voice was thin. He was looking past Jim, waiting for some sign from Spade. "You could be after the wrong man."

Jim caught Grady's look and knew now what lay behind him. He'd have to get Grady first, and hope the man behind him was a bad shot. . . .

"I don't think so," he said grimly. He took a step forward, his voice suddenly harsh and without patience. *"Use it!"*

Behind him Spade took a long step out of the alley and lifted his rifle. The shot from inside the alley spun him around, the rifle jarring one wild shot as it went flying from his hands.

Grady went for his gun as he saw Spade step out behind Davis—he never knew why Spade's shot missed.

Jim drew and pumped two shots into Grady

before the Overland man cleared leather. As Grady fell, Jim whirled, his muzzle swinging around to Spade fifty yards behind him.

But Spade was on his hands and knees. He was starting to crawl toward his rifle a few feet away.

Jim started to run toward him. But Len Petersen beat him to Spade. The tall gunman came out of the alley and picked up Spade's rifle before the wounded man reached it.

He turned to face Jim, a small smile on his lips. "Hi, Jim." He looked past Davis, to Grady's body lying in the street. He shook his head. "Still forgetting some of the things I taught you—like keeping an eye on your back."

Jim said stiffly, "Hello, Len." He eased his gun back into its holster. "I heard you were dead . . . firing squad in Santiago."

A few feet away Spade was crouched over his torn and bleeding arm. He stared at Petersen through pained, bitter eyes.

Petersen's eyes held a thin mockery. "Goes to show, you can't believe everything you hear."

Jim looked down at Spade, then back to Petersen. There was only one reason for Len's being here.

"Never expected you in Junction City," he said. "You always liked the hot countries."

Len shrugged. He reached inside his pocket, brought out a bronze medal with faded ribbons.

"I've had this with me a long time. It's yours."
He held it out to Jim. "General Morales said to
give it to you, just before they shot him."

Jim took the medal. "You came all the way up
here to give me this?"

"No," Petersen said quietly. "I'm working for
Overland now. I came here to kill you."

He looked down at Spade. "But I owed you
something for that time in Juarez. Bothered me
a long time." His smile was cold and without
emotion. "Now I don't owe you anything, Jim."

He tossed Spade's rifle to Davis and turned
away. Jim watched him go.

XVII

Sheriff Collins locked the cell door on a cursing Spade and went back to join Davis and Tom Shawn.

"I'll keep him here," he said to Davis. "But I won't guarantee he'll stay. Donovan will have a battery of lawyers down here—"

"He was with Grady when they killed Dick Rainer and shot Regis," Tom said angrily. "There're others who'll swear to it beside me!"

"Sure," Collins said. "I believe you. But Donovan will produce ten witnesses who'll swear in court that both men were somewhere else."

Tom's anger began to choke him. "You mean he'll get away with it?"

Collins shrugged. "That'll be up to a judge and jury."

Tom turned to look at the man in the cell. Jim put a hand on the angry man's shoulder. "Come on, Tom." He looked at Collins. "Just keep him locked up as long as you can, Sheriff."

Collins nodded.

Davis stopped by the door. "How's your deputy?"

"Better." Collins turned, looked out the window, he didn't want Davis and Tom to see his face. "Hank'll survive the bullet. But I don't think he'll be coming back to this job."

Jim said, "Give him time, Sheriff."

The lights were coming on up and down the street as they left the office. Tom glanced up at the gibbous moon. . . . He thought of Sanders and the rest of the crew working to undo the damage caused by Spade and Grady.

"I should be getting back," he said. "Sanders is going to need me."

"No," Jim said. "You're staying here."

Tom looked at him, puzzled. "If we're going to make Fort Cochise on time—?"

Davis cut him off. "Come on. Let's get a bite to eat first."

Ellen Saint put on her hat and coat in front of the small wall mirror and thought, without emotion, that it would be the last time she would be doing this.

Paul watched her from behind his desk. He waited until she started to leave, then he got up and intercepted her by the gate in the low railing.

His voice held a small, mocking anger. "What's the matter, Ellen? No good night?"

She looked at him. "Goodbye, Paul."

She pushed through the gate and started for the door and he followed her, taking her roughly by the arm.

"Goodbye?"

"I'm leaving, Paul . . . on the morning train."

He studied her, not believing. "Where?"

She shrugged. "Back where you found me."

He shook his head. "It's five years too late, Ellen. You can't leave now. I need you here."

She looked deep into his eyes, hoping . . . but she knew he was lying. "You don't need me, Paul. You never did. All I ever was to you was a front; all you ever did was use me."

"No." He tried to draw her to him. "I love you, Ellen."

She pulled away. "I thought you did—once. I was in love with you."

She turned and Paul watched her go and made no further move to stop her.

Jim Davis and Tom Shawn walked into the Trans-Pecos office fifteen minutes later.

Paul was back at his desk, a pile of papers in front of him. But his mind was not on his work.

He got up as they entered and walked to the railing. "Congratulations, Davis." His voice held a sneer. "An eye for an eye—a killing for a killing!"

He looked at Shawn. "It'll be Overland's turn tomorrow. More men killed. Is that what you want, Tom?"

Tom looked at Davis.

"Look at me, Tom—not him!" Paul's voice was harsh. "I'm in charge here—"

Davis cut him off. "Those wagons go out yet?"

"They'll be out in the morning," Paul replied. He started to turn away.

Davis turned to Shawn. "Get the warehouse men on the job. I want those wagons out tonight."

Paul spun around, his face twisting with anger. "Now you wait a minute, Davis. I'm running this office!"

"Not any more," Jim said. "I just made a change. Tom's in charge."

Paul walked back slowly to the railing, his face white. "*You* made the change. Who gave you the authority—?"

"Wire Mr. Simpson," Jim said curtly.

He turned to Shawn. "I'll be at Frenchy's Canyon, with the others. Clean out that warehouse. I want every pole, every roll of wire and every box of insulators on the way up there as fast as you can get them out!"

Tom grinned. "Yes, *sir,* Mr. Davis."

Donovan was in a grim mood when Petersen walked into his hotel room. Ranged along the wall, Wotjek and the others waited. Cigar smoke hung heavy in the stale air.

Petersen gave them all an offhand look. "Sorry, fellas. Guess you had a long wait."

Donovan's voice exploded harshly: "Just what in hell are you up to, Petersen? Who *are* you working for?"

Petersen walked to the table where a number of glasses and a whiskey bottle cluttered the walnut top. He picked up the whiskey bottle, shook it and turned to look at the battered Overland boss. His voice was mildly chiding. "You could have saved me a drink, Mike."

Donovan snarled, "After what you did today I wouldn't give you a decent burial!"

Petersen slowly set the bottle down and walked to Donovan. His eyes were suddenly cold and hard, but the big man didn't flinch.

"You shot Spade," Donovan said harshly. "Why?"

"Never could stand seeing a man shot in the back," Petersen answered. "Professional ethics."

A sneer glowed in Donovan's eyes.

"Besides," Petersen went on coldly, "I told you killing Davis is my job."

Donovan studied him, chewing on the soggy end of his cigar for a moment. "You saying you're taking the job?"

Petersen nodded.

Donovan wasn't convinced. "You just saved his life. Now you're going to kill him?"

Petersen's voice was hard. "That's what I said."

Donovan scowled, looked at Wotjek and the others. They were good in a rough and tumble fight, but not with guns. They couldn't go against Davis.

"All right," he said slowly, turning to Petersen. "You take care of Davis. Wotjek and his boys will finish the rest of it."

Petersen nodded. "We'll leave early in the morning."

XVIII

Ellen heard the front door slam while she was packing and a faint dread came into her eyes. She didn't want another scene with Paul.

She closed the bag and started for the door. There was a spare bedroom down the hall and she could wait until morning to finish her packing. . . .

Paul came in before she reached the door. He brushed past her and something in his face made her stop and turn back.

Paul reached inside a small alcove closet and pulled a trunk into the room. He acted as though Ellen were not there. He was in a hurry. He took a key from his pocket and unlocked the trunk and tossed the first layer of clothing aside. He reached in and took out a long slender bamboo tube and set it down beside him.

Ellen moved closer, staring.

Paul dug slowly in a corner of the trunk. His hand came out, holding a small capped jar filled with a thick, brown fluid. Very carefully he thrust it into his coat pocket.

Ellen said, "Paul—"

He turned and glared up at her. "Get out of here!"

She didn't move.

He reached inside the trunk again and brought up three small feathered darts. He slipped these into his coat pocket, dropped the trunk lid, and stood up.

He shoved Ellen aside and headed for the door. She ran after him.

"Paul! Where are you going?"

He looked at her. "Donovan couldn't stop Davis," he said bitterly. "But I will!"

She looked at the bamboo tube in his hand. "With . . . that . . . ?"

Paul's laughter held a savage ring. "The Indians of the Matto Grosso in Brazil kill jaguars with this. It'll stop Davis."

She backed away from him. "You killed Bill Davis and Orville with that?"

He nodded. "Kemp too."

Ellen's face was white. "You killed them . . . to stop one man? To ruin Warren Simpson . . . ?"

"He killed my father," Saint said. "Forced him into bankruptcy. It killed him, and my mother." He was looking at Ellen, but not seeing her. "I was in college when it happened. One day I had money and parents—and then I was nobody . . ."

Ellen's eyes filled with a sudden pity. "Paul," she said, choking, "killing won't bring them back. . . ."

He didn't seem to hear her. "Saint was my

167

mother's maiden name," he said. "Henry Corbin was my father!"

She tried to stop him. He pushed her away, slammed the door behind him.

Ellen stood for a long moment, staring blindly at the door, her eyes filled with tears. "Oh, my God," she said. "Oh, my God. . . ."

Jim Davis watched as the men on the cliff, using winch and pulley, hoisted the long pole up the rock face. It reached the top and swung in, out of sight from the men below.

Jim turned to Sanders, who was directing the work. "Moss get in touch with Tom yet?"

Sanders shook his head. "I think he's ready to test the wire now."

He stepped away from Jim, cupped his hands around his mouth and called to the men on the cliff. "We're coming up with the wire now, Joe."

The man by the hoist waved that he understood. Sanders turned to Jim. "If Tom keeps the poles coming, we'll make it." His grin was hard. "Not by much, but we'll make it."

"We'll need something to blast a few holes in that rock," Jim said. "I'll see if I can get in touch with Tom now."

He walked away from Sanders and the work crew at the base of the cliff, following the wire strung overhead. It skirted the gutted ranch house and went on down the valley. The poles were like silent sentinels, holding the long wire between them.

Bill had found a challenge in stringing wire, Jim thought, and now he understood why. He stood for a moment thinking of his own life, then he moved on to join the telegrapher.

Moss had set up a receiver and sender on a small trestle table at the base of one of the poles. He was testing the "tap in" wire, holding the copper end to the tip of his tongue. He made a face as the small electric current sent a tingling through him.

He made his connections, then looked up at Jim. "No break in the line," he said. "I can get through to Junction City."

Jim nodded. "Tell Tom to put a keg of blasting powder and some fuses on the next wagon."

Moss nodded, turned to his key. He tapped out his call signal and waited for a reply.

The incoming message ignored the usual "go ahead." It came in fast and urgent. Moss leaned forward, listening intently. Jim frowned. He knew code, but this was coming in too fast for him.

Moss looked up as the message ended. "That was Rawlins, sending for Tom Shawn. They've been trying to get in touch with us since last night. Paul Saint's on his way out here to kill you. That's what his sister told them."

Jim looked down the canyon road. If Paul Saint wanted to kill him, he'd have to show himself first. . . .

He said, "Acknowledge the message and send mine. I'm going to take a look in the barn."

Paul Saint lay flat on his stomach in the barn loft, peering through a crack in the warped boards. The bamboo blowgun was by his side.

It had been comparatively easy for him to get this far. Sanders and his men had worked through the night; in the dark no one saw him as he slipped along the canyon shadows and into the barn.

He had been waiting since dawn. Sooner or later Jim Davis would walk close. Close enough for a deadly feathered dart to reach him . . .

He squirmed closer to the loft door. Slowly, a fraction of an inch at a time, he pushed it open.

He could see Davis talking to Moss. He saw Jim turn and point to the barn and a shiver went through him. Now! He reached inside his pocket and took out the jar, uncapped it. He set it down very carefully and took one of the small darts from his pocket. His hand trembled slightly as he dipped the point into the gooey poison, then slowly eased it into the mouthpiece of the blowgun.

Behind him, among the scattered straw and torn

feed bags, something rustled. It might have been mice, or the wind or . . . Frenchy's ghost.

Paul didn't care.

Jim walked toward the barn. He was less than twenty yards from the door when Sanders' yell pulled him around.

The ruddy-faced construction man was coming at a run toward Davis. "Riders!" He pointed down the valley.

Jim turned.

He had expected them all morning. Petersen had said he would come, and Jim knew he would.

Sanders pulled up beside him, breathing hard. "Eight of them! But we're ready for them this time!" He turned and waved to the crew by the cliff. They scattered, each man picking up a rifle.

A hundred yards away Petersen raised a hand; the men with him stopped.

Petersen said something to Wotjek, then rode on alone, a tall man, easy in his saddle.

Jim waited. He had ridden with this man through much of Mexico, but he had never gotten close to him. No one, he thought, ever got close to Len Petersen.

The gunman halted his horse a few yards from Jim. He put his glance casually on Sanders, then on the armed men moving toward them from the cliff.

"Call them off, Jim," he said gently. "This is between you and me."

"Is that the way you want it?" Jim's voice was stiff.

Petersen shrugged. "No sense getting a lot of other people hurt."

Davis looked past Petersen, to the men who had come with him. "What about them, Len?"

Petersen smiled. "You stop me, Jim, and they'll turn around and ride back."

Sanders shook his head. "The devil with that, Jim! We've got them out-gunned! We'll take our chances—"

"We're shorthanded now," Jim said, cutting him off. "We can't afford to lose any more men." He looked at Petersen. "We were friends, once." His voice held a hard regret. "Does it have to be this way now?"

Petersen sighed. "I'm afraid it does."

He dismounted and slapped his horse on the rump; the animal moved away. He waited until the animal was clear, then he turned to face Jim, his hands by his side.

Jim made a motion to Sanders and the Trans-Pecos man moved reluctantly away.

Petersen said, "Sorry, Jim. But I needed the job . . ." He was watching Jim, facing the barn. A small surprised light flared up in his eyes a he went for his guns.

He drew and fired a split second before Davis,

but his shots were high, way over Davis' head. Then he staggered as Jim's bullets tore into him. He twisted and went down to his knees, dropping his guns.

Jim walked to him, not understanding.

Petersen looked up at him, managed a horrible, twisted smile. "Aw, hell, kid. Never could stand . . . to see a man . . . shot from behind . . ."

He raised his right hand to something behind Jim before he fell forward, on his face.

Jim turned.

Paul Saint's body was draped across the loft opening in the barn. He was still clutching the blowgun in his hands.

Jim Davis stood on the station platform with Ellen Saint. Her train was ready to leave.

"Yes," she said. Her voice was without emotion. "Paul killed your brother . . . and the others. He told me, last night."

"He wanted to break Trans-Pecos," Jim said, puzzled. "Why?"

"Paul's real name was Corbin," she answered. "Mr. Simpson will know why when you tell him that."

The conductor called, "All aboard," for the last time and Ellen Saint turned and went into the car. Jim waited until the train pulled out, then walked to the Trans-Pecos office.

Tom Shawn had been watching from the door.

173

He said, "The Overland crowd left town last night. Looks like we've got a clear run into Fort Cochise."

Jim nodded idly. "Yeah," he said. "Looks like we have."

He started to turn away.

"There was a girl here this morning," Tom said, "looking for you. Steve Orville's girl."

Jim paused.

"She said for you to stop by before you leave."

Jim considered for a moment. "I think I will," he said. He looked at Tom, eyes level, a bit of humor glinting in them. "I might even stay."

Tom watched him go up the street, then turned and went inside as the receiver began to chatter.

He knew it must be Jack Sanders. "All right," he muttered. "I'm getting the wire out as fast as I can."

Center Point Large Print
600 Brooks Road / PO Box 1
Thorndike, ME 04986-0001 USA

(207) 568-3717

US & Canada:
1 800 929-9108
www.centerpointlargeprint.com